Shadows of Winterspell

Also by Amy Wilson

A Girl Called Owl

A Far Away Magic

Snowglobe

AMY WILSON

Shadows of Winterspell

Illustrated by Helen Crawford-White

MACMILLAN CHILDREN'S BOOKS

First published 2019 by Macmillan Children's Books
an imprint of Pan Macmillan
The Smithson, 6 Briset Street, London EC1M 5NR
Associated companies throughout the world
www.panmacmillan.com

ISBN 978-1-5290-1896-7

3 5 7 9 8 6 4 2

A CIP catalogue record for this book is available from
the British Library.

Printed and bound by CPI Group (UK) Ltd, Croydon CR0 4YY

MIX
Paper from
responsible sources
FSC® C116313

For Aviva

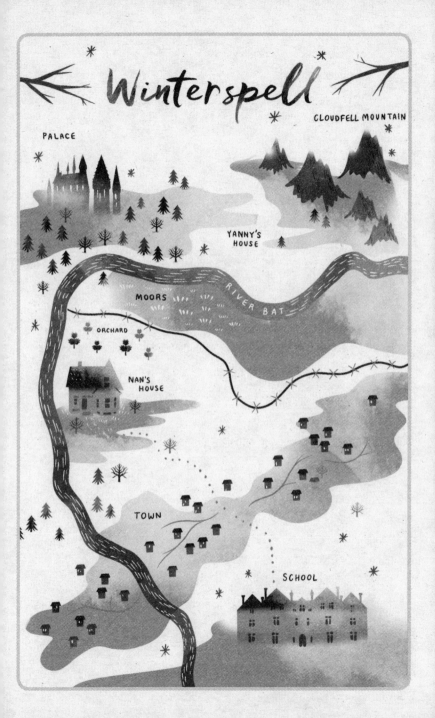

Daybreak

In the moment of dawn, the song of the centauride: a full-blown horn that rolls over misted grass. The forest is new, the first reaches of sunlight barely caught in the beads of dew that hang from every leaf and every blade. The centauride is down upon her knees in the deepest glen, still dark, and she pounds her fists against the ground to wake the trees, who wake the birds, who wake the world. Morning does not come easy; it does not come free. It comes with a fight – especially in the forests where the moon and her children like to dwell.

1

'Estelle!'

'Yes, Nan?' I try to sound calm, but her voice often sends a little wire of shock through me. She has a knack for catching me just when I'm doing something I know she wouldn't approve of, like using ancient words of magic to make strawberries come in October. I pull a dishcloth over their growing red hearts and turn from the sink as she billows out through the fireplace and swirls in front of me, slowly gathering into her usual shape.

'This house is a mess. When was the last time you dusted?' she asks, brushing at the front of her dress. 'The whole place needs a thorough going-over.'

'*I* think it's OK,' I say, looking around, fingering the silver acorn at my neck. I mean, it's a bit cluttered, and actually I really can't remember the last time I dusted, but I don't mind, and I'm the one *living* here, after all:

Nan's a ghost, and my parents are only distant memories.

Nan was the one who brought me up – with books and gardening, with forest explorations, and adventures through the trees. We spent so many days on the outskirts of the forest, watching the creatures from afar, while she told me their secret ways and warned me never to go beyond our well-trodden paths without her. We tended our orchard and played hopscotch on the crumbling patio by the back door. She made jam sandwiches and told me tricksy tales of fae children and enchanted treasures, of goblins and of the palace locked deep in Winterspell Forest, lost to all, and she taught me how to look after our home. Nan is pretty awesome, but she's been a ghost since before I was born, and it's hard for her to do much these days.

When I was younger, she was a little more solid; she could cook, and she could hold me. But as I got older, she got thinner, and now she mainly hovers over me, making sure I'm doing what I'm supposed to be doing: keeping the herb garden going, harvesting the vegetables, making the jam with the damsons and gooseberries, feeding the chickens. Oh, and learning the old spells that keep us safe here, hidden between the realms of fae and humanity.

She says we belong with neither, not while the Shadow King reigns in Winterspell.

'How's the spell-work coming?' she asks now, hovering over the kitchen table, where the books are heaped in a pile. 'Oh, darling, you should look after these better – some of them are centuries old! Irreplaceable!'

'I know,' I say, shoving them to one side, away from the breakfast honey spill. 'I am doing my best. But it's lonely.' There's a long silence. Her grey eyes stare into mine, unblinking. 'So I wondered if you'd had the chance to think about, um, if it would be OK if I . . . you know . . .' I pull out one of the chairs and drop into it, putting my chin in my hands and staring at Nan, making my eyes as wide as they can go.

'Oh no you don't,' she says with a firm shake of her head, coalescing into the chair opposite mine. 'That trick won't work on me, my dear. The answer is no.'

'*Please*, Nan.' My eyes start to prickle.

'It's just not a good idea, Stella,' she says. 'I'm sorry, but don't you have enough on your plate with looking after this place and your lessons?'

She smiles, but it doesn't reach her eyes – she's afraid for me. We don't go far from the house any more. The forest is forbidden now that she's weaker, and we hide as much as we can from the real world too. I get it – or at least part of it. The world of magic is not a sparkly love-fest; it's a dark, fickle wilderness. And we know that better than most. Nan's taught me the spells to keep our house protected from the fae, and we have a whole library full of texts on fae and magic, so it is a fairly full-time job, keeping the boundary live and looking after everything else.

But I'm lonely, and I'm tired of hiding. The chores keep me busy, and books keep me company, but it isn't enough. I need people. Friends. The feeling keeps growing, no matter what I do. And so that's at the crux of the campaign I've been waging for the last few weeks. Since I'll never be welcome in the world of the fae, I've decided – I need to be part of the human world. I need human friends.

I want to go to school.

2

The nights are getting longer, now that summer's over, and tonight the moon is hiding behind stubborn clouds. The forest behind the house is thick with the ethereal light of the creatures Nan taught me about, the ones in my favourite books – centaurs and fairies, dryads and goblins, and water sprites who can curse with one flick of their tails. Brambles catch at the silver wire fence hung with charms, which divides the forest from our garden. I pluck a blackberry, checking it over closely before putting it in my mouth.

'Shouldn't have done that,' says Peg, fluttering before me, his red wings a blur.

'It was on our side . . .' I say, savouring the sharp tang of the berry.

'The roots aren't. You'll be corrupted.'

'I'll be fine.'

Peg sniffs. He's an imp, and his favourite form is a

small red bird with a golden beak. Whatever guise he's in, he's very beautiful, very vocal, and regularly very annoying. He's a real stickler for the rules.

He'd be horrified at what I did earlier.

Because I really did it. A shiver of apprehension runs up my spine just at the thought of how I've disobeyed Nan. Peg peers around at me.

'What was that? Are you poisoned?'

'No! I was just thinking about something.'

'Dark thoughts, ominous tidings – it's the berry!'

'It's not the flipping berry! Now go and see what you can find out there . . .'

Peg is Nan's familiar, and nowadays our watch imp; he scouts out the forest for trouble. I mean, there's always trouble, but he'll find out if anything's about to start trouble here. There's a magical boundary, just at the point where our fence divides the garden from the green marshland that leads to Winterspell, and the creatures in the forest don't cross it, but sometimes I hear them at night, faint whispers of parties, the clamour of hooves, the high-pitched call of fierce, flying things. I've never managed to actually see them from so far away, no matter how many nights I've spent curled up on the cold windowsill, watching.

Our family ruled them all, long ago. We were the kings and queens of fae. But the Plaga came when I was two and killed my mother within a day. And my father was lost too – to illness, and to grief. With her dying breath, my mother called Nan back to the world of the living and charged her with bringing me up, safe and well. Nan saw the danger in the forest, and so we fled, and here we are, hiding from the forest, while the Shadow King's legions grow stronger, day by day, fighting with the fae over the fate of Winterspell. We keep to our house, with all our books and wards and spells that apparently protect the rest of the human world from his creeping shadow magic.

When I was small, we ventured into the forest – under Nan's glamour so that none of those creatures could sense us – and we searched for the palace, which is the heart of the Shadow King's power. But we never found it. His darkness has warped the land, made it impossible to find even for us. And every time we went in there, the shadows were harder to hide from; they gathered thick about us, and the fae who fought them had to fight all the harder on those days. So we left. I could see how it upset Nan, to walk away from Winterspell and all the fae, but we only made it worse for them. We couldn't go very far – her power, the thing that keeps her with me, is tied to the magic in the forest. So we have spent all these years hiding between the forest and the town. Nan used the last of her real magic to glamour the whole house, and us inside it – when I look in the mirror, I am human.

Only, I'm not. It's just that her spell made a shield that disguised me. And it's been there so long that we don't know what I'd look like without it. Every fae is different, and sprites like us have many forms. Would I have horns? A tail? Nan has pointed ears and moon-round silver eyes, but I am a mystery. She says it doesn't matter; that I am Stella, whatever shape I'm in. She says I can find friends in books, and that is true. And we have many, *many* books, so I have spent days and weeks caught up in adventures with the characters between the pages. But the longer I'm here alone, the more I crave my *own* adventures. My own *friend*.

I mean, Peg is a friend, of course. But he's very small and a bit flighty, and he can be pretty superior. I haven't got the courage to tell him yet what I've done. It's going to be a Big Deal.

I phoned the school.

After I talked with Nan and realized she might really never let me go – and that the forest may be out of my reach for as long as I live – I really did it. I checked the perimeter, set the charms swinging, silver sparkling in the low sun all along the fence, and muttered the familiar words Nan taught me that keep the fae and the shadows of Winterspell out of our home – our sanctuary: *'Not mediocris, nor twisting umbra-form, shall pass between these acies, for they mean domum; our domum be our sanctum, free from inimicus be.'*

And then I made the call we've been arguing about for so long.

It wasn't easy. First, I sprinkled salt in a circle around the kitchen table. (If Nan had come back, she'd have known I'd hidden myself from her and Peg on purpose, but I could have just told her I wanted some privacy. She wouldn't have known what I was really doing.) Then I picked up the phone. Put it down. Picked it up again. Dialled. Cursed my shaking fingers and wondered what on earth I was going to say.

'Broadmere Academy – how may I direct your call?'

That was as far as I usually got. I'd tried many times . . . and put the phone down. But I had already told my reflection that today was the day, and the face that looked back at me had beamed with hope and possibility.

'Um. I'm new to the area. And . . . how do I register?'

'Register?'

'To come to school.' My cheeks blazed.

'Oh! Well, usually your parents would apply, through the usual authorities.'

'Oh.'

Silence. And then a long sigh.

'One of those, eh. Name?'

'Estelle. I mean Stella. Stella Brigg.'

'One minute . . .' Sound of papers shuffling, a lot more sighing. *'OK. Hold,'* the woman's voice snapped.

The phone line crackled, there was a pipping sound. I stared at the phone. It wasn't really going how I thought it would, so far.

'And why are your parents not making this call?'

Well, you see, my mother died long ago from fae plague, and my father didn't die of it, but he did not survive it whole either, so now he haunts Winterspell from his hidden palace, and all his shadows are at war with the fae.

He is the Shadow King, you see.

'Um, it's just my nan. She's in the other room . . . She said I should do it to . . . teach me independence.'

I winced, crossing my fingers as I realized I should have pretended to be my mum or something. Why do I always have these thoughts too late?

'*How curious,*' the voice said after a short pause. '*Come along in the morning, and perhaps we can sort something out. There are usually various formalities, but I suppose you'll be coming alone? As part of this independence drive?*'

'Ye-es . . .'

'*Very well. Tomorrow – 9 a.m. sharp.*'

The line went dead. So tomorrow morning, everything will change. Everything has *already* changed, actually; I've never defied Nan before.

I watch Peg flute up into the darkening sky and head back inside, where only shadows greet me. There's a storm building in my chest. Nan appears as I pour hot water into a mug with fresh mint from the garden, but I can't speak, can't even meet her eye right now. She frets around me in a spiral of motion, and I wish she would sit down – a real body in a real chair. I wish she could hold me; that I could feel her paper-soft hands on mine, like I used to. Sometimes, here, my own skin aches for the touch of another human being – even just by accident. A nudge, a flick, anything.

Tomorrow, that might even happen. The storm

inside me becomes a bright spark of hope. I hold my hand up in a silent goodnight as I head upstairs, and she holds hers out to meet it – except, of course, they don't touch.

The Imp

The imp is a master of disguise and can shapeshift at will. Clever, naughty, not entirely trustworthy, they are the preferred familiars of many fae for their ability to spy and their fierce loyalty.

FIGHT – 7

FLIGHT – 10

MAGIC – 10

DISGUISE – 10

3

It's hard to leave in the morning. I stare at myself in the mirror for a moment, thinking of Nan's old glamour spell and whether there are features I should be hiding, but I can't see anything out of the ordinary: brown hair, brown eyes, round face. Me.

I huff at myself and flit down the stairs, hastily undoing charms to get out of the door and the gate, then whispering the familiar words to restore them behind me. Then I charge off down the lane on my own, for the first time, while Peg flutters and spirals over my head demanding to know what I'm doing, chirping about duties and responsibilities. He's so panicked, it would be easier – kinder – just to forget the whole thing.

But if I do that now, it'll never happen. I'll just spend my whole life trapped in the house. I look back at our home, glowing pink in the early morning light, nestled between folds in the foothills that lead to Cloudfell

Mountain, where all things are wild. Winterspell Forest snakes from the moorland that borders our garden and makes a broad swathe around the mountain, and even from here, I can see the sparks and the sweeping shadows that mean something in there is having a good old fight.

'Stella, please!' Peg says, fluttering next to my right ear as the lane gets wider. 'Where are you going? Please stay! What will I say when Nan asks after you? What about the spiders?'

'You can just tell her the truth.' I sigh. 'I've gone to school. She'll work it out anyway. And I'm not going to stay just because you're weird about spiders. I don't know why you're so scared of them.'

'They're itchy,' he says darkly. 'And they don't follow the rules. They shouldn't be able to get into the house at all with all your wards set. And you won't be here to get rid of them! You'll be at this *school* of yours.' He flies faster so that he's in front of me, a blur of indignation. 'I can't believe you're doing this, after all those discussions – all those times she said no! What if you don't come *back*, Stella? What if it swallows you up, and you never come home?'

'I will come home, lovely Peg,' I say, holding up my

hands and cupping them around his tiny warm hum. 'I promise.' Dark eyes stare into mine and see everything in an instant; there is no hiding from Peg. 'Do you see?'

'I see you give your promise honestly,' he says, breaking away from me with a huff. 'Can't account for chance, though!' he calls back, heading back towards the house.

I adjust my bag on my shoulder and turn my back on home, heading towards the river path and the town that creeps up slowly from isolated old houses to small redbrick terraces, to the main roads of towering grey.

I've never done it without Nan, and we haven't done it for so long. It feels colder and stranger now, and the pedestrians I pass all have their heads down, swaddled in scarves and hats. It's still early, and the sky is misty with fine rain. I pull up my hood. Soon, I'll be at school. And the other kids will notice I'm new, and I'll have to smile and talk and be human, and I really, really wanted that – but right now, it's a fizzy kind of terror that makes my feet go faster, over cracked roads and past a noisy construction site where vast yellow machines dig their teeth into the cold, dark earth.

I keep to the shadows as I cross the town streets, my head down, feet quiet on the slippery pavements. Cars swoosh by through the puddles, and the bakery on the high street is already open, its blue sign gleaming. The smell draws me in, and before I know it, I'm standing in the doorway, wishing I'd brought some money with me. I ate porridge and packed my lunch this morning, but it's just a yellow pear, a carrot and a piece of cured sausage, and suddenly I'd do pretty much anything for a hot pasty, or one of the raisin-studded buns on the shining glass counter.

A couple of men brush past me on their way out, clutching paper bags. They don't appear to register me, but the woman behind the counter stares, her brow furrowed.

'Sorry,' I say, taking a step back. We don't shop here. I shouldn't have stopped. I shouldn't be here at all. I should go home now. Feed the chickens, because Peg will probably forget, and curl up with a book by the fire. Why would anyone want anything else?

'Hang on,' says the tall fair-haired woman. 'What did you fancy, lovely?'

'Oh, nothing . . . I, um. It smelt good.' I force a smile. 'I'm just . . . heading for school. It's my first day.' I clench my fists in my pockets. It is my first day. I am doing this.

'Ah,' she says. 'A bit of nerves, then. I thought you

looked worried. You'll be fine. They get all sorts at that school – some real characters . . . You don't need to worry.'

'Thank you,' I manage. 'I should go.'

'Wait a minute,' she says, drawing my eyes up. There's a sparkle in her blue eyes that makes me wonder, just for a second, if she has a little magic. Some people do. A bit of fae blood, passed through generations, or an affinity with the words in books of magic. The closer you are to fae, the more you open your eyes to it and the more you can do. That's what Nan says, anyway. 'You can have a teacake, if you'd like.'

'Oh, but I didn't bring any money,' I stammer.

'That's why I didn't say *buy*, my dear,' she says, shaking her head. She reaches out and plucks one of the buns from the top of the pile on the counter. 'Call it a first-day treat; you look like you could use one. Horrible out there today, and that forest was fair howling last night.' She shivers. 'I think I'll have one too, come to that. I'll toast it for you. Butter?'

'Um. Yes, please.'

She cuts two of the buns in half and slides the pieces into a gleaming toaster. Then she thrusts her hands into massive oven mitts and turns to rearrange the trays of pastries in the oven on the back wall. I watch her, shuffling my feet and hoping it won't make me late. When the toaster pops, I jump half out of my skin. She shakes her head at me with a little smile, removing the mitts and buttering the teacakes with a practised hand.

'Here,' she says, putting mine into a paper bag and handing it to me. Her eyes sparkle again as she takes a bite of her own. 'That'll get you warmed up. Have a good day, lovely.'

'Thank you,' I say, past a little lump in my throat.

She nods, and I back out of the shop, clutching the bag between my cold hands. I hold it like that for a couple of streets, and only when the school looms into view do I take my first bite. I can't believe I'm actually here. The teacake tastes as good as it looks, and it soothes me while I loiter on the edge of the pavement, getting up the courage to make the next move.

4

The school is a rambling collection of redbrick buildings that rears up on the east of the village, behind a complicated road junction of traffic lights and underground tunnels. The River Bat, which starts in the mountains behind our house, has grown wide here, and it rushes past, caught behind the concrete wall that leads to a squat bridge.

It took me a while to cross the road – I didn't know which way to go, and the pedestrian tunnel was dark and damp. It's a relief to be out of it now and in the right place, staring up at the sprawling jagged skyline and the huge old brass bell that swings in the tower over the main school building. I shiver as the sun disappears behind it.

BROADMERE ACADEMY reads the shining green sign on the metal gate. There are points on the ends of all the letters, like spearheads. I smooth down my good dress – a faded dusky-blue one that Nan made for me to grow into – and retie my boots. It's suddenly quiet, all the noise of the town behind me, and I have no idea what I'm about to get myself into. From out here, I can't see anybody. No students on the steps; no movement in the windows. Nobody loitering out here like me.

I take a big breath, push open the gate, and head up the steps.

The wide glass doors open automatically as I loiter outside them, looking at my own reflection. My heart is tripping; my fingertips numb. I take a breath and step into a small lobby. There's a silver box on the wall and a button that says *PRESS FOR ATTENTION*, so I swallow hard and press it.

There's a long silence. I stare at the silver box, wondering whether to press the button again, and then there's a buzzing noise and a woman's voice breaks out, making me jump.

'*Yes?*' it demands.

'Uh, my name is Stella Brigg. I called yesterday . . .'

'*Come in*,' says the voice.

There's another buzz, and the door opens out into a bright reception area with a ridged navy carpet and a long, pale wooden counter. A tiny woman with short curly hair and a sharp chin sits behind it on a stool, peering at me.

'So you're our *trial* student,' she says with a thin smile. 'Welcome to Broadmere. I am Mrs Edge.'

'Hi.' I manage a smile, sidling up to the counter. On the ledge behind it is a computer, a phone, a tray of papers and a huge silver spike.

'What papers do you have?' Mrs Edge asks.

'Uh, none. Sorry . . .'

'Ah, one of *those*,' she says, tilting her head with a small frown. 'And you're all alone in the world? No parents?'

'They, um . . . They died when I was small. But I do have my nan.' I don't mention that she's a ghost. 'She's . . . housebound.'

'I see. Well, I'm sure you'll find yourself in good company here. Sign here.' Mrs Edge thrusts a clipboard at me, tapping at the bottom of a heavily typed page, where there's a dotted line. 'I take it you're from the forest. You can write?'

'Yes.'

The reference to *the forest* unsettles me, and I don't quite know what she means by *one of those*, but it doesn't

24

matter, because I can hardly concentrate on anything she's saying. I try to read the page before me, but my heart is thumping so hard, it's difficult to see straight. I catch the words *behaviour* and *discipline* but not much else.

This isn't how I thought a school would be. It doesn't seem like the ones in books, where there are corridors full of kids, and fish fingers for lunch, and kindly librarians. Maybe there will be once I'm through this bit, I reassure myself. There's a pen caught in the clip at the top of the page. My hand shakes, and the snap as I pull it out makes me jump.

I wanted to come to school, I remind myself. This is the school, and I'm here now. I take a deep breath and finish the signature, handing the clipboard back to Mrs Edge. Her eyes flick from me to the page, and then she whips the paper off the board and thrusts it on to the gleaming silver spike. I flinch.

'Wait over there,' she says, indicating a row of plastic chairs along the wall next to a wide door with little green wire hexagons in the glass. 'I'll get somebody to show you to your first class.'

'I didn't see anybody outside,' I venture. 'Are the other students already here?'

'The school day begins at 8.40 a.m. sharp,' she says. 'So they are already in their classes. There will be plenty of bustle to come, don't worry about that!'

'OK.'

I settle back into the chair, clutching my bag on my lap. My calf muscles twitch with the urge to run out of here, so I shift in the seat, screwing myself more firmly into it. Mrs Edge gets a brass call bell out of the top drawer, sets it on to the counter, and then slams her hand down on to it twice, two clear notes sounding out. She returns the bell to the drawer and folds her hands upon the counter, staring at the door.

Who would have heard that, through the door and the whitewashed walls?

Just a moment later, though, a slender boy with longish chestnut hair opens the door.

'Yanny,' she says, looking him up and down.

He is a bit scruffy. And a bit . . . *something*. He catches me staring and gives me a glittering smile.

'This is Stella. She is here with us for a trial period, while we sort out paperwork. Could you take her up to your form room and introduce her to Miss Olive, please?'

'Yes, Mrs Edge.'

Yanny stares at me while I unpeel myself from the plastic seat, picking up my bag with numb fingers. He indicates for me to go before him, and the door slams behind us, the sound echoing through a wide hallway with a polished wood floor. There's a staircase leading down on the left, and another leading up past a row of windows on the right. The sun blazes in over a green sports field, where a group of kids are playing what looks like hockey.

I stare at them. I didn't bring any sports clothes with me – I'm not sure I even own any. There's so much I have never thought of. So much I'd never imagined, even with all the books on schools I've read. My stomach is churning with nerves, and my head thuds with the beat of my heart, but there's also a little glow wickering deep within me, because I really did it – I got this far.

Let the adventures begin, says a little voice inside my head, and I hold on to it, even as Yanny leads me through a maze of white-walled corridors.

This is school. This is normal. This is what I wanted.

5

I don't know about normal schools, but I don't think this is one.

Here, there is a great staircase that shimmers like a trick and leads up to an old, ornate wooden door. Silver charms hang from the sweeping curved banister that remind me very much of the ones I set at home.

How can that be? Am I imagining it? Is it the berry Peg warned me about yesterday, making me see things? I train my eyes on Yanny and ignore the staircase, focusing on everything else that's going on around us. So much buzz and noise and heat and tripping down steps and through corridor after corridor, it's a relief when finally we stop in the doorway to a classroom where the sun streams through wide glass windows, and bags and coats are flung about like autumn leaves.

What was that staircase? Did I really see it?

'What do those stairs lead to?' I ask in a whisper

as I follow Yanny into the room, trying to sort of hide behind him. The room is warm, and my coat itches, and there are at least two dozen other kids in here, most of whom are chatting in low tones while a woman with grey-streaked hair glowers at a computer screen.

'What?'

'That weird staircase, with all the charms.'

'Charms?' He frowns. 'I'm not sure which staircase you mean. Probably just more classrooms.'

But now he's staring at me, and his eyes are just a little too wild. That staircase is definitely hiding something. Can there be magic here, at the school? This nice, ordinary school, which I came to because I wanted to know what it was like to be truly human, in a truly human world? Nan's told me that some humans have an affinity for magic, but surely not to the extent that they'd hang charms? Why would they even need them? Unless there are fae here?

Why would there be fae in school? The very idea is laughable.

Yanny lifts his brows. 'You OK?'

'Yep. Sorry. Fine!'

'Miss Olive, this is the new girl, Stella.'

His voice seems to boom, and all of the easy

29

conversation stops as everyone looks at us. At me.

'Good morning, Stella.' The teacher looks up from her screen and smiles, standing. '8E! This is Stella . . . ?' She looks over at me.

'Brigg,' I whisper, my skin prickling as I look around at all the curious faces.

'Stella Brigg,' she announces. 'I'm sure you all remember your first day, so I expect you to be welcoming!' She turns back to me. 'Take a seat with Yanny; he'll see you through. I'll print out your timetable now, once I can get the thing working . . .'

'Thank you,' I whisper, darting with Yanny to a table at the back of the room, my face burning under all the intense stares.

'Sure you're OK?' Yanny asks, staring even harder while I try to get my coat off. It's become some sort of woolly mammoth and wants to smother me entirely.

'Yes,' I say, finally yanking it off my arms and letting it fall in a heap on the floor behind me. Some of the kids are still looking. I take a deep breath and hook my ankles around the chair legs, fixing my eyes on the table. Slowly the room settles, until it's just Yanny peering at me.

'I'm fine,' I say.

He's still staring.

'What?'

'Nothing,' he says. 'Nothing at all. Welcome to Broadmere.'

His smile doesn't quite reach his eyes, but my heart lifts a little anyway because here I am, in my first ever classroom.

After a while, Miss Olive hands me a timetable, which is a grid that seems to have been written in code, and then a bell starts clanging, and everyone rushes out.

'Where are we going?' I ask Yanny.

'Lessons!' he says. 'Let me see . . .' He looks at my timetable. 'You're with me for science – come on.'

I follow him gratefully, through the clatter of bodies that yesterday I craved so much. I had no idea how loud they would be, or how close. I get jostled and bumped and nearly go flying down the stairs, but somehow, keeping Yanny in sight, I make it in one piece to science.

The teacher, Mr Hocking, hands me a thin blue-covered book and barks my name to the class, before starting his lesson on force and trajectories. I clutch the book and squeeze in next to Yanny, barely noticing anything else about the class in my rush to get rid of my coat and find my pencil.

It's a heads-down kind of lesson. Mr Hocking has

sharp blue eyes and an even sharper tongue, so there's no talking. I look over at what Yanny's doing, and he indicates the massive text book between us.

'That one,' he whispers, pointing to a triangular diagram.

I have no clue what any of the writing means, but I copy it all down anyway, and then Mr Hocking draws a simplified version up on the big board and begins to go through it all.

It's a huge relief when the lesson is over, I'm not sure I like Mr Hocking, but when I turn to Yanny to find out where we're going next, he looks hassled.

'Uh, right,' he says, glancing at my timetable. 'I'm going in the other direction. You have maths . . . Zara, don't you have maths next too?' He turns to the girl next to him, who nods.

'Mr Goodenough?'

I look down at the timetable. The piece of paper is crumpled already, and I don't even know which bit to look at.

'Here,' she says, tracing her finger down one of the columns. 'M8, Mr G. You're with me. Come on.'

I look up to thank Yanny, but he's already gone.

'Oh, he does that,' Zara says. 'He's nice enough, but not what you'd call steadfast. He's gone off to have one of his special lessons . . .'

'Special lessons?'

Does she mean magic lessons? Is he going up that weird, magical-looking staircase? I squint after him, but he's disappeared already.

It can't be that.

'Honour-student thing,' she says. 'No such luck for us.'

I'm a little bit in awe of Zara. She fills the space with her words and just her general presence. She's a head taller than me, her dark hair spools down to her waist, and her eyes are honey gold, narrowing as she gives me a quick, appraising glance.

'So, where've you come from?' she demands, swinging out into the corridor, scattering smaller kids and bowling through them.

I hurry after her, hunching my shoulders, making myself small. 'Um. Just home.'

'Home?' She turns and arches one eyebrow. 'What, like home-schooled? Wow. This must be a bit of a change for you, then.'

'I wanted to come to school.'

'Well, you chose a weird one,' she says. 'I only started last term myself, and there are lots of things going on that I haven't worked out yet. Including Yanny and his secret lessons. Come on.'

She sweeps off into a classroom and sits at the back of the class, which is a relief, because it turns out being the new girl is a bit of a challenge when you're used to being in your house alone with a very small imp and a ghost nan. There are just so many *people*. So many warm bodies, rushing and nudging and staring and whispering.

Zara has a lot of stationery. She pulls it out of a huge fluffy pencil case and lines it up on the table. Biros, highlighters, sparkling pencils, and a huge blue rubber that says *For Big Mistakes*, which makes me smile.

I get out my old striped pencil, scratched and scored after a run-in with Peg, and the folding wooden ruler I found in the study. Zara looks at them and then at me. And then with a tiny sigh, she carefully pushes all her stuff over so that it's in the middle of the table.

'Help yourself,' she whispers, as a man with white hair in the shape of a candle flame walks in and perches on the edge of the table at the front of the class, pink socks winking between trousers and shoes.

'Thank you,' I whisper.

She smiles, as yellow exercise books are handed out from the box at the front of the class. The teacher looks at me with a frown.

'You must be Stella.'

'Yes.'

'Welcome,' he says, as the rest of the class stills to listen. His voice is round and shiny as a new conker. 'I'm Mr Goodenough.' A shiver of energy rushes through the room. He walks over to Zara and me, a yellow book in his hand. 'Here you go.' His eyes glint as he stares at me, handing over the exercise book before striding back to the board at the front of the class. 'Division!' he says, picking up a pen.

Zara copies a complicated sequence of numbers and symbols into her book with great care and a number of different pens, so I follow her lead.

The cafeteria is even busier than the rest of the school and full of noise. There's a lot of laughter, and talk, and charging about with trays and bags and coats. I sit with Zara at a table beneath the window, and she gets out a plastic box with lots of different compartments. There are grapes, small wedges of flatbread called barbari, a little pot of yogurt-and-cucumber dip, a packet of very thin crackers, called crisps, and a wrapped chocolate biscuit.

I get out my pear and my old bit of sausage, feeling a bit embarrassed. Zara looks over and purses her lips.

'Do you live in Winterspell Forest?' she asks.

'No,' I whisper. 'My house is quite close by, but not actually in the forest.'

She looks like she's going to say more, but then Yanny careers into the cafeteria and swooshes through all the other kids to land with a clatter and a grin at our table.

'How's day one going?' he asks, sliding into the chair opposite us. He pulls a battered tin out of his bag and opens it. Tiny golden pastries nestle in waxed paper along with a shiny red apple and a wedge of dark, sticky-looking cake.

'Yanny has the most ridiculous lunches.' Zara sighs. 'But he is very good at sharing.' She gestures to her own box, and Yanny takes some of the crackers, shoving his tin towards us.

'Help yourself,' he says with a smile. There's a pull in the air when he does it, which makes the world darken for just a second. My chest aches. And then it's gone, and the buzz of the cafeteria returns.

But it was there for a moment; I'm sure I didn't imagine it. Magic. Forest magic, dark and alluring. How can that be? He's human. Isn't he? I stare at him, and he stares back, and Zara reaches over and takes one of the pastries, putting it whole in her mouth.

'Mmph,' she says, closing her eyes. 'So good . . .'

'I don't have much to share,' I say, looking down at my meagre spread. I wish I'd thought to bring more. I could have made a cake . . . or brought some of the good cheese.

Zara shakes her head and charges off, returning quickly with a knife. She smooths out my paper bag and lays everything out, sausage and pear neatly divided. The pastries collapse into layers of buttery goodness in my mouth, and Zara's salty crisps are delicious, too. The pear from our orchard is smooth and tastes of summer. One of Nan's favourite stories is the one where her human grandfather built our home and planted the orchard, and of how he'd trade with the creatures in Winterspell Forest: golden pears for the rich, dark berries that made his favourite wine.

Of course, that was before he met the fae queen and became a part of their world. Long before even Nan was born, and an age before the Shadow King – my father –

began to destroy all the goodness there . . .

I stare at Yanny. His food tastes incredible, but the way it dissolves makes me wonder if there's magic in it. If he lives in Winterspell, he must know all of its secrets. He doesn't look much like a fae warrior to me. Especially not with pear juice all over his chin.

'So,' begins Zara, scrunching up the crumb-festooned bag and throwing it with an expert flick of her wrist into the nearest bin. 'Are you going to tell Stella about your *secret* lessons?' She grins as she says it, but there's an edge to her voice, and Yanny's dark eyes glint.

'They're not secret,' he says. 'Just extra languages – that sort of thing.'

I think it's meant to fend me off, but it doesn't, because a lot of magic is about language. Many spells are written in Latin or Ancient Elvish, and there are books full of Greek and Norse in our library. One of Nan's favourite lectures is about the study of language being the most powerful there is.

'I like languages,' I say. 'Who's your teacher?'

'Miss Capaldi,' he says. He closes his lunch tin and shoves it back in his bag, just as the bell rings. 'Come on. We have art together.'

'If you find out,' hisses Zara as we head off through

the corridors in his wake, 'you will tell me, right? I've been trying to get it out of him for weeks, but he's immune to my questions. You already have him rattled. Maybe he can see you're on to him. *Are* you on to him? Do you know what's going on?'

'No idea!' I manage. And it's true, but this whole thing is disconcerting. If Yanny is a creature from the forest, if there's some kind of magic going on up there, I can't share that with her. The fae and the human worlds don't mix. Or at least, I didn't think they did. Here, anything seems possible, and it's not what I wanted on my first day. I wanted a *normal* school, not one with magic on the top floor, and secrets that seem to make awkward spaces between friends.

Even as I think it, I smile. Because however complicated today might have been, it's been a day. A day of school. Of lessons, and lunch, and new friends who talk and share, even though they hardly know me at all.

No matter what Nan might say, I know I won't regret that.

6

Nan is furious. I round the corner to our house, and she is billowing out of the chimney in a great dark cloud of worry and fear. All the lines I've been rehearsing, the stories I've held in my head to tell her, vanish completely. I loiter, walking slowly down the lane. I need time to work out how to talk my way around her, and my mind is still working through everything that happened today.

It was chaos. Loud, and hot and completely bewildering. I hardly remembered to breathe for much of it, and I still don't know anything about any of the lessons, or how to read the flipping timetable. The smells and the sounds still clamour in my mind, and that fizzing feeling of nervous excitement I had this morning is still there in the pit of my belly.

But.

I grin. It was fun. And I made friends.

Peg darts up to me as I bend down to pick up an

acorn, searching through dried amber leaves for its cup.

'Well, I hope it was worth it,' he says, whirring about my head.

I sigh and plonk myself on to the ground, cross-legged, catching him in my hands and holding him up to eye level. He blinks. His presence is so small, and yet it fills me up. He's been with me for as long as I can remember; there is no part of my life that he couldn't sing.

Except today.

'Peg, I think it *was*,' I say through a sudden lump in my throat. 'I'm sorry. I'm sorry that it upset Nan, and if it caused trouble for you, but I wouldn't change it. I *won't* change it!'

'You'll go back?' He tilts his head.

'Tomorrow.' I look at the dark earth, packed and dry beneath the leaves. Peg flutters to my knee as I start my search once more. 'And all the days after that.'

'*Every day?*'

'Not weekends. Just Monday to Friday. Nan will get used to it,' I say, finding the pitted acorn cup and holding it up with a grin. It's bigger than the silver one around my neck, but even so . . . they're such small things that the great oaks grow from. 'She will, Peg. She loves me. She'll see that it makes me happy . . .'

41

Funny how such a tiny creature can make such a sound of deep disapproval. Peg manages it, and then he launches off and away into the forest.

He keeps secrets. All the time, off in the forest, and he'll never tell me anything about what's really in there. I want to hear news of the centaurides and the sprites, and the mirror lake where golden fish speak bewitching tales to unsuspecting passers-by, just as they do in all Nan's best stories. I want to know of the shadows, of my father. But all Peg ever says is that the forest is fair, and frightful wild besides.

I tuck the acorn into the earth by the side of the path with a little wish, touching my own silver acorn and hearing Nan's voice, years ago, on one of the days I yearned for more. 'It is here,' she'd said, reaching out and touching it with pale fingers. 'It is not whole, and it is not the shape we may have hoped for, but there is family here, and if you hold it tight, Stella, you cannot lose it. It will grow . . .'

'I said *no*!' Nan howls when I finally gather up the courage to walk through the back door. She's writhing around the kitchen table, clasping her mist-thin hands together.

I dump my bag and lean up against the table.

'How could you, Stella? After all these years of you and me, all the trust, all the lessons . . . How could you just abandon it all?'

'I haven't! I can still do lessons here. You can't just keep me locked up forever. What happens when I'm older? Did you even think of what would happen when I grew up? Am I supposed to live my whole life here alone?'

'Of course not,' she snaps, coalescing into her true shape. Nan shape. She reaches out to me, and I feel the chill of her touch, see the regret on her face when it makes me flinch. 'I wanted to keep you . . . keep you safe for a while longer. That's all.'

'I am safe,' I tell her. 'There are hundreds of kids there. It's a normal school!' I push away the thoughts of magic and secret lessons. 'I did maths, and English, and PE, and I shared my lunch with some of my classmates. How can that be wrong?'

'It is wrong if you go against the wishes of your family. I am not holding you to others' standards – I am holding you to ours! We are the keepers of this house, the only ones who stand between the shadow forest and the human world. The time will come when that will

43

mean everything. Isn't that enough excitement for you?'

'It isn't exciting! It's silver wire and books and rules and old, musty things that aren't even *alive* any more!'

'Well, I hope that's not me you're referring to,' she mutters after a shocked silence.

Peg is being a small golden lizard. He stares down at us from the wooden beam where copper spoons hang, catching the firelight, and I feel horrible. Like I turned myself inside out, and they can both see all the messy bits that are normally hidden within.

'What do you mean by *the time will come*, anyway?' I ask after a while.

'The forest grows, and so does your father's darkness,' she says. 'His shadows seek to swallow the world whole. One day, you will be the one who stands in his way.'

'Me?'

'Of course you!'

'We can't even get into the forest, Nan. We have no idea where his palace is any more, or even if he's still there!'

'Legend says you will face him – I've told you so before. When you are grown. This house and all the magic we have gathered here is headed for that day.'

'Well I'm not doing it. I don't know how to face him.

I don't even know what I'd be facing! Besides, every time we've tried to get close, all we've done is make it worse. I need to have more than just legends, Nan.'

'*Just legends*,' she splutters. 'All the world is made of legends!'

'No! It's made of people!' I shout. 'I need this. I can keep our barriers strong. I can study *and* make the house safe. I will be here when the time comes. But I need to have this too.'

'It's a bad idea,' she says.

'Can you stop me?' I demand.

'Well. I could lock up the house so you can't get out . . .' Her eyes gleam.

'I could unlock it.'

'With magic?'

'I do know a spell or two.'

'I should think you do! I've been teaching you for long enough. And you've been reading the books, no?'

'Of course I've been reading the books. The books are all I've had for years!' I fling myself into the old armchair by the fire, and she floats to hers opposite.

'And your old nan,' she says with a growl in her throat.

'And you . . . and Peg. But you're not . . . You're not *people*, Nan!'

'People.' She sniffs. 'I think I'd take a ghost or an imp any day, over people.'

'I do. I have. But I really want to at least know some people before I decide they're all rubbish.'

She sighs, and a ravel of her essence puffs out like smoke.

'Perhaps it will be a relief, not to have you trailing around like a lost cloud,' she concedes after a moment.

My heart leaps, and I grin, dancing my feet on the floor.

'A trial period,' she says, raising a finger. 'And you must tell me *everything*.'

So I do. I tell her about the lessons, and how the corridors fill with charging crowds and flapping bags. I don't tell her about Yanny, or the magic I felt in him, or about the hidden corridors. I don't really know anything about them, anyway.

'And there's a lot of stationery,' I finish. 'And . . . good lunches.'

'I didn't go to school,' she says. 'We had a tutor, my brother and I.' She folds her arms. 'What's this about good lunches? We don't have good lunches here? Cheese from the cellar and sweet apples? Bread from Mrs Mandrake?'

Mrs Mandrake delivers food every Saturday morning. It's a standing order Nan has, and she's paid up to infinity, she always told me. The bread Mrs Mandrake makes herself, and there's milk and golden butter from her cows. Sometimes, there is elderberry cordial; sometimes, she'll bring cake. She stays and drinks tea and looks out of the window towards the forest and talks about when she was a girl and she discovered the fae magic in Winterspell, and Nan rescued her from the lake where the mer-fae like to sing. Nan loves to see her; she puts so much energy into *being* here when she visits that I barely see her on Sundays.

'They had crisps.'

'Well, you have brown potatoes *and* Mrs Mandrake's salty butter. And you have a whole house of wonder. You don't need crisps. Or special stationery. What *is* special stationery?'

'Bright-coloured rubbers, scented pens, sparkly things . . .'

'Oh the world does love a sparkly thing,' she says darkly. 'Until they see what lies beneath.'

'What?'

'We can ask Mrs Mandrake to bring you supplies if you need them,' she says then. 'I want happiness for you, Stella. I just didn't think it would take this route.' She exchanges a look with Peg and shakes her head. 'Humans. Let's hope they're as good as you think they can be.'

'Your grandfather was human, and he wasn't so bad, was he?'

'Hmph.' She folds her arms. 'Make a list of all these stuffins you think you need. And then chores. And an omelette for tea, with some of those lovely brown potatoes . . .' Her voice drifts as her body pales into nothing. She doesn't stay as long as she once did, back when I was smaller. She isn't so solid. She's wearing out.

One day, maybe she won't come back at all.

I swallow hard and pull an old notebook towards me and start my list, and I think about tomorrow, and Mrs Mandrake's visit on Saturday, and I fill my mind, and I pack my heart with all the sparkly things I can imagine, and Peg flutters about me, warm and full of song.

That night, the chores are easier. The chickens – Onion, Basil and Salt – seem pleased to see me; the carrots come out of the loose earth without a fight; and the silver wire that holds the boundary between our garden and the edge of the forest is a bright moonlit line, hung with charms and tatters of spells from generations past. I can touch them when I'm here. My parents, my grandparents, the reality they left behind. Paper they wrote on, folded and tucked into glass baubles, enchanted copper bells and tiny vials of blood and thistle-down, all collected by Nan and used to hide our house from the fae and the shadows that live in Winterspell.

I trail my fingers through it all and let my mind fill with who they were. My mother, the artist; my father, the mechanic. Fleeting images of them appear in my mind as I touch the essence they left behind: moving scenes of laughter and tears and dancing between endlessly tall trees. Splashing through the river, the drift of snowfall. Snatches of their lives before the Plaga, caught in tiny glass jars. My father had a plaited beard with copper strands that fell to his waist. My mother had pale hair that flew out like a starburst around her head.

'I went to school today,' I tell the moon, hoping that somehow my mother will know it. I recall my day, as if she can see straight back into me from wherever she is. Yanny, and Zara, and chaos and crisps.

'You won't leave for good?' asks Peg in a tiny voice, fluttering over the wire and making it hum.

'No, of course not. This is home.'

'Good.' He stares at me. 'Don't you forget that. I'll keep it safe while you're gone – but you must always come back, Stella.'

'For the day I'm grown?' I sigh.

'For me!'

I hold out my hand, and he curls in my palm, a golden lizard once more, and we go back in together. Then he and Nan boss me about the kitchen until I've cooked a pretty good omelette and just-soft potatoes, and I light a candle on the table and crank up the radio, and Nan tells one of her old stories about the centaur who fell in love with his reflection and was only saved from drowning by the silver birch who threw her seeds into the water to break the spell. The scrape of cutlery is only mine, and it is only me who can clear up afterwards, but right now, it doesn't feel so lonely. It feels like home.

That night I don't stay up staring across the field towards Winterspell. I don't sit on the windowsill while shadows dance between the trees, wondering about the fate of the fae in there, or what my bitter, broken-hearted father is doing. I close the curtains with a shiver and think about tomorrow.

But my dreams are tangled things of forests that

grow thick along school corridors, and strange creatures chasing me down endless staircases, and in the morning, while I gather pears and cheese, and I butter the last of Mrs Mandrake's soft, dark crusted bread, the anticipation of the day sends fizzles through my veins. And there's something else. A little fear. What is Yanny hiding, with his special lessons and the way he makes the air change? Could he really be fae?

No matter, I tell myself. Whatever he is, I'm not about to miss out on school, after all this, and now that I've got Nan's blessing. I dart through the door before she can take it back, and let myself be soothed by the reflection of the yellow sky in the slow-moving river, the mist still clinging to the moorland that bounds the forest, the weight of my bag on my back, the acorn around my neck that means family.

I've got everything I need.

Nothing I can't handle.

7

Zara is waiting for me at the gate, the only still point amid the mass of kids' bodies streaming through the vast wrought-iron gates. A little rush of joy squirrels through me as she raises one hand in a wave. As if I wouldn't notice her. As if I wouldn't stop.

'OK?' she asks, as I get close. 'It's nice that you're punctual. Normally I wait for Yanny, but he's always late, and I really hate being late.'

'Should we wait for him, then?'

'No – he doesn't like it much. I can't help telling him he's late, and he already knows he is, so it's not the best start to the day. Let's go in, and he can sort himself out.'

It's funny to think she doesn't like going in on her own. She seems so confident; she glows with a kind of ready-for-anything energy.

'Are we in the same form room? I didn't see you there yesterday . . .'

'Oh, I think you must've come in late, I was running an errand for Miss Olive. She has trouble with printers. So, about Winterspell,' she says, as we head in, her voice low. '*Do* you live there? What can you tell me?'

My heart thuds. Why do all things lead back to Winterspell?

'Uh, I don't know. Like what?'

'I wanted to go for a bit of an explore in there, but my mum says it's forbidden – something about pollution in the water and ancient trees that fall without warning. And the kids at school say it's haunted. Which can't be true?'

She stares at me as we head up the steps to our form room. Unblinking owl eyes.

Can you start a friendship with lies?

No.

'Ah, I don't know about *haunted*, exactly,' I say. 'But my nan says we should avoid it.'

'Even though you live so close?'

I hold in a sigh. She's not going to give up so easily, but it's the last thing I need this morning. My worlds are getting tangled already; with every step I take towards humanity, Winterspell creeps further in.

'We used to go in there sometimes,' I say, 'but it's

creepy, and it's got worse. Strange noises at night; weird lights flashing between the trees.'

It was supposed to be a little bit of truth to put her off, but now her eyes are glowing. 'Really? Wow. I do believe in ghouls, you know. My Mamani has some *very* creepy stories about them. And if you were a dark spirit like they are, then an old forest like Winterspell would be the perfect place to hide . . . I'm not sure I'd want to be there, but everyone's different. Mum says it's the pollution that makes the mist rise when the sun sets, but I don't know. And Yanny won't tell me anything.'

'He lives in there?' I ask, my voice thin at the thought of the dark spirit who does hang out in Winterspell, somewhere. My father, who does not love strongly enough to find his way through.

'Well, I think he does. He gets very strange about it when I ask him.'

'Where do you live?' I ask, taking my coat off as we find seats in the form room.

'In town,' she says. 'It's OK. I didn't really want to move, but Mum got a new job, and so . . . here we are.' She stares out of the window. 'We lived in the city before; it feels quiet here. Everything's a bit strange. Mum says it's just because it's new, but I don't know. I think it's genuinely weird.'

I grin as Miss Olive starts reading out the register. 'It's definitely weird.'

'Zara Nassar?'

'HERE!' she shouts in reply to Miss Olive, before lowering her voice again. 'I don't know why Yanny won't talk about it.'

'Maybe it's not weird to him. If he lives there.'

'I s'pose.' She sighs. 'But there are definitely secrets in that forest, and up that weird staircase.' Her face grows serious, and she plays with the cuff of her jumper. 'I do not like secrets, Stella.'

'Here,' I say, raising my hand as Miss Olive gets to my name. I look back at Zara. 'But doesn't everybody have secrets?'

'You talk far too much sense for this time on a Friday morning,' she says. 'Everybody might have them, but that doesn't mean they *should*!'

Just then, Yanny rushes into the form room. Miss Olive glowers at him, and he gives her a smile that I swear radiates straight to her. She checks his name off her list with a gentle shake of her head, and then the bell rings, and we all pick up our stuff and head out again, catching him in the tide and swirling back out into the corridor.

'G'morning,' he says, untangling himself from the knot of kids heading in one direction, to come with us towards science. 'Missed you at the gate, Zara.'

'No you didn't.'

'I don't know how it happens,' he says, charging up the steps two at a time. 'I leave at the right time – Ma hassles me enough . . . It just seems to take too long to get here.'

'Maybe you dawdle,' she says. And then, with a wink at me: 'Maybe it's the spirits in the forest, slowing you down.'

He falters on the landing for a split second as she charges up past him, and she doesn't notice how he blanches, as if she hit him in the stomach. It's there and gone in a blink, and then he rushes on after her, bag swinging, bright as ever, but the feeling remains in my belly all through the morning, and I can't look him in the eye, even when we have art again without Zara. It's just me and him sitting at the end of a big table, and the teacher is late, so everyone's chatting, except I don't know what to say to him.

'How's it going?' he asks.

His freckles glow under the artificial lights; it's dark, and the clouds are stormy outside, and the whole place suddenly feels claustrophobic. Every lesson is a different textbook, a different teacher, a different classroom down a different corridor. I've got lost every time I've looked for a loo, and I don't know anything. I take a deep breath in, filling my chest, and breathe it out slowly, lowering my gaze to the old wood table with its scored lines and crossed-out words.

'Stella?'

'It's different,' I say. 'I wanted it so much. I still do. But it isn't what I thought it would be.'

He doesn't say anything, and it takes me a long time to look up from the desk. When I do, he's staring at me.

'Sorry . . .' I start, but he shakes his head.

'I was trying to imagine how it feels. You really never . . . You never went to school before?'

'No.'

'So what did you do?' his curiosity is suddenly needle-sharp.

I shrug. 'It's just me and Nan at home, and Peg, my . . . my pet. There's lots to do, but . . . it was lonely.'

'You'll like it here,' he says. 'You'll fit right in. I can feel it.'

He smiles. There's that flicker of magic, only this time it doesn't tug at me. It soothes, like the flame of a candle. I remember when Nan used to glow like that, before she faded.

Our last visit to Winterspell was the winter I turned ten. That was when I knew for sure what Nan was. She'd talked to me for years about the legends of the fae, and the Plaga that strikes every few generations, and that this time took only my mother. About how the grief of my father, a fae king in his prime, had become a visceral thing that birthed the shadows that have blighted Winterspell ever since.

How she'd hidden me so that his shadows, grown into their own power over all this time, would not be able to reach Winterspell's last future hope: me.

She never told me what she was.

I thought she was flesh and blood, a sprite just like me. Like my father, the tree sprite who I barely remembered, just a blur at the edge of my mind – stern one minute, laughing the next. Like a storm in spring. I wanted to know him, even as the very idea of being close to him now terrified me.

That night, we stole between the glowing stalks of

winter trees at sunset, and she held me close as ever and used her magic to shield us, and we watched as tiny, bright figures leaped between branches. Spiderwebs gleamed like copper wire, and the trees flexed their roots beneath the hard earth with deep sighs, and there was singing in the distance. We skirted around them, watching, listening, and we trod on our familiar path, searching once more for the cursed palace.

But as we went, the way grew colder. Frost gathered in every nook. Trees hung with bright daggers of ice. And between their stark branches, the shadows came. They were wolves, and men eight feet tall, showing their teeth and claws, howling into the grey winter air. We pushed on, for only if we reached the palace could the king be raised – maybe even brought back to himself. Back to me. But the shadows were bolder. They were snakes upon our path, and bats in our hair, they were great monsters, and when they touched me, it hurt. With every breath, they took something from me – and as they took, they grew.

The terror overtook curiosity.

'Nan,' I managed, when I could barely move. She turned back, and horror whickered across her face. She rushed back to me, howling, cutting a swathe through the shadows.

And then the thundering hooves of the centaurs approached, and the shadows turned at the noise, and we scrambled back, hidden from the fae beneath Nan's glamour. Our breath steamed as we tripped on tangled roots, and the barren sticks of willow reached for our clothes, as roiling dark clouds withered through the trees. A great stag bellowed, rushing through the forest by our side, and when I looked at Nan, she was barely there at all.

'Nan,' I hissed, pulling at her hand, but my own went through hers. 'Nan!'

'Hush,' she whispered, and her eyes were dark hollows. 'Don't let him hear you now, Stella. Come after me. Come, *come*, Stella – as fast as you can.'

She was like bright smoke herself though, her form twisted as we flew back through the forest, and while I got scraped and tripped, the branches snapping with every pace, nothing touched her at all.

'Stop,' I whimpered, stumbling as we got out on to the moorland that ran up to the orchard at the back of our house. 'I don't know . . . Who *are* you? What's happening?'

'Keep *coming*, Stella!' she wailed, turning and clutching at me. Her fingers gripped my wrist, and they were cold and hard. 'I'll tell you – I'll explain – but we must run. We must keep going until we get home!'

Home.

The word flashed through me. What was home, on the edge of this wilderness? What was home, with this Nan who grew thin as cloud, until I could see the stars through the outline of her body, as her hand gripped mine, and we flew over uneven ground to the silver wire of home, as we ran from my father's hordes of fear and malice?

That was the night I discovered Nan was a ghost. I knew, after that, there was nothing for me there, in that forest. My father was only a memory, impossible to reach, and Nan had used everything she could to hide us from his shadows. That was why she'd got so thin, and she never really recovered from it. That was how the magic of that other world soured. It's a terrifying, wild place where nothing is as it seems. Where I am not welcome. And it's the real world – the warmth of the humanity I read about in my favourite books – that I need.

That was the night I started to dream of school.

8

Mrs Mandrake is late, and I cannot help but flit, watching for her. First from the windows, and then in the orchard, where I decide it's finally time to pick up the fallen apples. Nan laughs at me when I collect the basket from the top of the washing machine, and Peg hops in, a tiny brown mouse huddling into the twist of willow. I grab a carrot and chop it small, and when Onion bustles up to me, I scatter the pieces across the grass.

'You spoil them,' Peg says, winking up over the side of the basket as Basil and Salt rush up to grab their share. 'They're not even laying at the moment!'

'They will,' I say. 'In spring.'

'Not much use until then.' He sighs. He does love a good egg. 'We could always have chicken for dinner . . .'

'Peg!'

I turn to the orchard, a dozen stocky apple and pear

trees, their leaves golden brown now and starting to drift to the ground. In the summer, I climb up and read in the branches of my favourite tree – the one closest to the boundary, where the fork between two branches is wide and smooth.

The apples are small and sweet, their skin a dusky pink that bleeds into pale yellow. I leave the ones that have already been half eaten by insects and gather the rest, carefully dropping them into the basket. Peg organizes them as I go, so that by the time we've finished, they look like a rolling sunrise.

'Very pretty,' I say, carting them into the kitchen, just as the front gate squeaks, setting off a row of tiny bells over the fireplace. 'Mrs Mandrake!'

'She'll be happy you're going to school,' says Nan, settling into the armchair and stoking the flames with a wave of her hand. 'Always on about it, she was.'

'I didn't realize,' I say, picking up my list, unfolding it, and folding it again.

'Oh, she did it on the quiet. Little hints – worried you'd be lonely.'

'Imagine that,' I say, watching through the window as Mrs Mandrake bobs around the side of the house before knocking on the kitchen door. She pulls a trailer with her, loaded with food, and I rush to help unpack it as Nan gathers all her strength to look like a real, flesh-and-blood person. There's bacon, and chestnuts, a jar of cocoa, a fruit loaf and orange juice, a bag of oats, dried pasta, and a basket of tomatoes and shiny bell peppers.

'I'll put the kettle on,' I say when we're done putting it away, and Mrs Mandrake sits at the table opposite Nan and looks down at my list. Her brown eyes are dancing when she looks up again.

'What's this about scented pens?' she asks with a smile. 'And a calculator? A PE kit! Did you win her over, Stella?'

'No. She was flagrantly disobedient and off she went without permission,' Nan says. 'And she's determined to continue, so we're calling it a trial period.'

'Good job,' Mrs Mandrake says. 'About time she got herself out there in the world.'

Nan huffs, and Mrs Mandrake winks at me. And then she dashes back out to her truck to get the crumpets to go with the tea, and I light the fire. I love Mrs Mandrake's visits.

The warm feeling stays long after Mrs Mandrake

leaves for her other errands, and even after Nan has disappeared again. Peg stays close, and after we've eaten all the chestnuts and about half the fruit loaf, I head out in a bit of a dream to set the charms.

The night sky is soft, stars flicker between scattered clouds over the moors, and the wind is singing through the silver wire. Peg has taken his true form for the night: a gleaming bronze imp with tiny red horns just above his ears, and curling, nimble hands and feet.

I love it when he's just being an imp; I could watch him for hours. Only he doesn't like it too much, being peered at. He bounds up now and sits on my shoulder and folds his arms and scowls, when suddenly the charms begin to ring.

'What're they doing in there?' he mutters.

'What they always do, I suppose,' I say.

'No. Nothing stays the same in there for long.'

'I thought you went back in sometimes. You know, as our watch-bird?'

'Watch-bird,' he scoffs. 'Well as to that, I did,' he says. 'For a long time. But it's changed in the last weeks. It's darker now, and I am not welcome. The shadows are everywhere. Most of the good folk spend their lives fighting or plotting escape.'

'There's a boy at school . . . I think maybe he lives in the forest.'

'Don't tell Nan,' he says, but he doesn't sound surprised. 'She'll worry. It's one of the things I discovered, last time I was in there. Some families send their children to the school so that they get a human education and live in the human world, away from the forest. They started when the shadows took over, but only some are able: those who can pass for human, and those who are good at glamouring. I guess your boy is one of them, and Nan's glamour does the job for you. For now . . .' He looks me up and down, as if to check it's still working.

'I didn't realize that was happening. Why didn't you say anything?'

'These things are for you to discover. You made your choice when you started at the school.'

'And you were cross, so you thought you wouldn't tell me something so important?'

'Nobody ever said the school would be a safe place, Stella. Nobody said it would be a good idea. You decided to go anyway. And now you are discovering things for yourself. Isn't that what you wanted?'

'I always thought you'd tell me if something important

happened in there. I know you like your secrets, but—'

'But nothing. You need to use your own eyes, and your own judgement. If I truly thought you were in danger, I would tell you. It was always a tricksy sort of place; now, even the skies are darker for it.'

I look at the sky over Winterspell and notice for the first time that the stars above are glowing red.

'Shouldn't we do something?'

'You and I?' He grins, his sharp teeth glinting. 'And Nan? Against all the king's army of shadows? We tried that, Stella. Your presence in Winterspell only made them fiercer. You're doing what you can, with all your learning.'

'That doesn't help the fae in there, though.'

'They are fighting,' he says. 'And mostly, they are winning. The fae have always loved a good battle.'

I stare into the gloom.

'Aren't we ever going to try again, then?'

'Oh, we will,' he says. 'When the time is right.'

'So for now, we just have to *wait*? I don't know what we're waiting for, Peg. It's stupid to live so close when we can't go in there.'

'It is not stupid!' He draws himself up with indignation, a spiral of smoke escaping his nostrils.

'Nan's power is connected to Winterspell; that's why we stayed so close. And one day, the time will be right, Stella. You will go in there, and you will find the palace.'

'Well let's just hope that's before the shadows have spread too far to be contained,' I say with a shiver, a little bit cross and a little bit relieved. As much as I want to march in there and find that cursed palace and stop the shadows' sprawl, the thought of fighting through them again is terrifying, and so is the idea of my Shadow King father. I cannot imagine ever feeling ready.

Peg doesn't say anything, because there isn't a right thing to say. We both know it's happening. Young ash trees encroach further every season, their grey bark catching the moonlight and making stripes across the ever-diminishing moorland that stretches between the forest and our perimeter. And with them, come the shadows.

9

I hit the dusty old books over the rest of the weekend, while storms rage about the house. There's little else to do. Nan is recovering from Mrs Mandrake's visit and only really emerges at mealtimes to make sure I'm eating my greens, and the rain drives down into the soil and makes a swamp of the garden.

I want to know more about fae curses, and the grief of kings, and how we're going to fight the shadows. Something like this must have happened before, somewhere. But the books that line the study shelves aren't exactly organized, and many of the covers are so worn, it's impossible to make out the writing along the spine.

Peg pretends he's scandalized by the turn of my study. He thinks I should leave the whole thing alone, but I can tell he's not really that cross. He loves the old books – a little too much, actually.

'Peg!'

'It just smelt *so* good,' he manages around a mouthful of paper. It smokes a bit in his mouth.

'I might *need* that page!' I stare at him. 'What's got into you?'

'Change,' he says. His eyes glow. 'It's uncomfortable – good for the soul, I always thought.'

'Well I don't know about that, I'm trying to find some actual *solutions* here. What if you've just eaten the spell I need?'

'It was a diary entry about tatting lace,' he says, smacking his lips. 'Was that how you were planning to wage war against the forest?'

'I don't know! I don't know what lace . . . tatting is, and now I never will.'

He belches and doesn't look sorry at all. 'Lace tatting is the construction of particularly durable lace. It's useful for making doilies.'

'Doilies –' I spread my hands – 'are what, exactly?'

'Those little frilly mat things that go under sugar bowls.'

I huff at him and pull my book closer. 'Please don't eat any more. You never know. Maybe lace tatting is really good for anti-shadow armour . . .'

'They're not clouds, Stella. They have teeth. Real teeth, real claws. You're going to need more than a lace doily against all that.'

'OK,' I say.

For a few minutes, there's silence while I try to translate some old Germanic that seems to be hinting at something to do with the blood of a yew tree. But I'm too distracted to concentrate.

'Peg?'

'Yes, dear Stella,' he replies from the nearest pile of books, reaching into a small copper bowl of pumpkin seeds.

'Why are you going along with this? You didn't exactly like it when I started school.'

'Change,' he says, tossing a bunch of seeds up into the air and sending them spinning with a gesture of one small hand. He huffs, and they form a smouldering ball, which fragments piece by piece as each finely toasted seed falls into his waiting mouth, until only a crescent-moon shape remains.

I breathe a few spell words, and the crescent becomes a fiery bird that swoops down over our heads before collapsing into ash on to the table. Peg watches me.

'Sometimes, it's inevitable, and you may as well just

go along with it. You wouldn't have tried that spell before. Last week, you wouldn't have called the school. Last *year*, the shadows hadn't spread the way they have now. We are drawing closer to our futures, Stella. May as well read up on it.'

'Very sage advice,' I say. 'Coming from a paper-eating, seed-shuffling imp.'

He grins.

But it's not quite funny. The way he said it, the flicker in his eyes, there was something dangerous there. Something different, even in him.

Peg was Nan's familiar when she was alive. When my parents died, Nan was called upon by my mother to look after me, and he came with her. I don't know that she could have done it without him. And I don't know why my mother didn't linger as a ghost. Why all this happened in the first place. I have wondered. More than wondered – I have felt it burst from the hollow place deep inside that hurts, when the dusk is yellow, and the swifts gather in the sky in tumbling, swooping tides, and summer is over. A why and a where and a how – but mostly the *why*. *Why* did it happen? *Why* is Nan a ghost and my mother isn't?

Nan says it's because my mother was a better person than she is; her spirit went straight where it was supposed to go. I wish it hadn't gone anywhere. If she had survived the Plaga, everything would be different. My father did survive it, but not really. His illness, combined with his grief, cursed everything in Winterfell. *Why?* Why did he descend so deep into shadows that he couldn't even see me? Does he even remember I exist?

So many questions and no answers. Even if I had answers, they wouldn't bring my family back. That's what I tell myself when I check the wards one last time, trudging through the wind and the rain, bitter-cold fingers touching every glass vial, every brass bell, every silver coin. I know the pattern of them so well, I could do it in my sleep. Sometimes, I do dream of them. But in my dreams, my mother walks with me. Here and now, it's just me, and the fog of my breath. And a glimmer, a flicker of red light blooming between the trees, and the darker shades that nestle between. There's a howl, and the enraged call of a stag. Thunder of hooves, flash of movement, and then the slightest whisper of song, low and haunting . . .

I used to fall asleep to those songs.

I hold my breath, straining to hear more, my hands still on the silver wire—

'Stella! I made hot chocolate!'

It's a rare treat, Peg's hot chocolate. He does something to it that makes it spicy. I catch up the last charm, a small wooden acorn, and breathe the old words of protection over it, satisfied when it flickers with the amber mist of spell-magic. And then I dash back through the puddles to the warmth of the kitchen, and Nan is there, curled into her old blue armchair with the frayed cushions, bickering with Peg.

When she sees me, her eyes light up. I shut the door behind me, shuck off my boots and my coat, and pull on my thick wool socks, then I dive into the other deep chair by the fire – this one of soft green cord. Nan sits opposite me, and in the flickering light, she's as vivid as any living thing. Peg stretches out on the mantelpiece with a deep, dreamy sigh, and I reach for the wood bench and my hot chocolate, curling my cold, brittle fingers around the heavy mug as Nan clears her throat to begin.

'Long ago, when the stars were young, and the world was greener . . .'

I lift my knees and curl them under me, and I let her words do their magic.

10

Monday morning, and Nan doesn't exactly wave me off from the front door, but she does flutter about making suggestions of more fruit while I make my lunch, and she wishes me a day without drama. I hunch into my coat and shift my bag on my back, and bird-Peg flies over me in loops and whorls, showing off to the rest of the dawn chorus, until I reach the river road.

Mrs Mandrake stopped by to drop in my supplies last night, and though Nan made a point of tutting, I could tell she was curious as I unwrapped paper parcels to find a new pencil case, a neatly folded PE kit and a whole hoard of sparkling things: silver pencils, miniature star erasers, a pencil sharpener in the shape of a rainbow cloud.

'Very fancy,' Nan had said after a while.

'I picked them out myself,' said Mrs Mandrake, looking satisfied as I unwrapped a flexible blue ruler and a tube of glue.

'Thank you,' I'd said, and her eyes twinkled, but she'd not stay for tea, thank you – there were other errands to be done.

Now, I race up the steps to reception and dart past Mrs Edge. And then people turn as the door clatters shut behind me, and my footsteps slow. I don't know quite what to do, without Zara or Yanny by my side. It's fine, I tell myself. I can't be with them all the time. But I've noticed that some of the other kids sometimes stare at me a bit, and they're doing it right now.

Zara says it's normal for a new kid, and she's glad I've taken over the role. But it makes my skin itch, so I've taken to staring back at them when they do it.

Then.

I smile.

A really slow, impish sort of smile.

And that normally makes them stop staring, even if it's just to turn to the next person and start whispering. I wonder what they see. I wonder if it'll always be that way. Would people have stared the same if I'd started in year seven, instead of partway through year eight at the grand old age of twelve? If I'd gone to school at four, like everybody else? Sometimes, I wish Nan's glamour upon me would slip, just a little, so that I could see the sprite in me – but right now, I'm glad of it.

I head for the form room, hoping Zara won't be long. I should have waited for her – I understand better now why she waits out the front in the mornings. I finger the new pencil case, wondering if she's waiting for me somewhere, and then she bursts in, late and flushed.

'OK?' I ask as she slides into the chair next to mine, Yanny following after her.

'Yep.'

'She hates being late,' Yanny says, shaking his head in mock disapproval. 'And it wasn't my fault this time . . .'

'Mum's started night shifts, so I had to get the bus, and I miscalculated,' she says. 'That's all. It won't happen again.'

'How was the bus?' I ask.

'Smelly,' she says. 'And it seemed to go *so* slowly. Anyway, I made it. How was your weekend?'

'Good.' I think back to my studies with Peg, and Mrs Mandrake's visit, and the rain. 'Wet.'

'You went shopping!' she says, noticing my new things. 'Mum and I went back to the city to see some friends, and Dad took me bowling –' she rolls her eyes – 'which we were both rubbish at because we'd never done it before. Then we went for pizza, which was pretty good. Anyway, we only got back last night . . . What about you, Yanny?'

'Fine,' he says, offering nothing further.

Zara tuts and starts investigating the contents of my pencil case, and I look up to see one of the girls staring. I stare back with a nice smile.

'What are you doing?' Zara asks, catching me at it again later in our English class.

This whole new-girl thing is getting old.

'She's giving them *the imp*,' says Yanny.

'What?' Zara looks baffled.

We both turn to look at him.

'*The imp*. Staring at someone, smiling, giving them the creeps.'

'I'm not sure the creeps is what I was aiming for . . .'

'Well, you weren't being friendly,' he says.

'They were staring at me first!'

'This is a very strange and immature conversation,' Zara sniffs. Then her eyes sharpen on Yanny. 'What's that about imps? Are they real?' She leans in closer to us. 'They're *real*, aren't they! I *know* there are strange things going on here . . .'

'It's just a turn of phrase!' Yanny says, shaking his head and picking up his rather battered book.

'Nope. Try again.'

'It's a thing,' I say, feeling my skin heat. 'You know, like an impish grin. You've heard that before . . .'

Zara frowns, but she doesn't get a chance to say anything more because Mrs Arnott is giving us all a stare that has nothing to do with imps, and we spend the next half-hour writing about the downfall of humanity in *Animal Farm*. Well, I do, and Zara does. Yanny spends most of it pretending not to stare at me, until I give him the imp.

'Where did you say you live?' he whispers, as soon as we sit down in history. His eyes glow, and there's a tiny little pull, deep in my chest.

Magic. He's using magic on me.

'Just outside the forest. How about you?'

'On the other side.'

'The other side?'

'Of the forest.'

'I didn't say which side I was on?'

'Well, we clearly don't live on the same side, so it must be the other side.'

All the time, that little glow, that smile, that pull of power.

There are different kinds of magic, Nan says. There's the kind that comes from within, when you are a creature of fae, that is in your blood and your soul and in everything you do. And then there's the kind you can learn from books – words of power that can be used to make spell-magic with just a little bit of heart. I can do a little of both, same as she could. But Yanny's definitely using the first kind right now – I'm sure of it.

'Stop it,' I whisper.

He pulls back. 'So you *do* have magic.'

'Enough to know when it's being used on me!'

'You should be enrolled.'

'No I shouldn't! . . . Enrolled into what?'

I stare at him, while the teacher starts talking about Joseph Lister, but he doesn't answer. My hand reaches for a pen, and when Mr Allen starts making notes on the board, I follow the rest of the class in writing them in my book.

Yanny does really have fae magic.

'What should I be enrolled into?' I ask him again as we make our way to the cafeteria.

'Can't tell you if you won't do it.'

'How can I do it if I don't know what it is?'

He spreads his hands. 'Frustrating, isn't it.'

'How would I? When?'

'Meet me in the science corridor, after school.'

'What about Zara?' I ask, as I spy her through the glass doors of the cafeteria. She's already grabbed a table, and she's shoved all her stuff into the two seats beside her, a fierce look on her face. 'She hates not knowing things. She'll hate it even more if it's the two of us . . .'

'I know,' he says. 'But we can't tell her.'

'Why not?'

'It's part of the enrolment. One of the rules.'

'But I haven't enrolled yet.'

He pulls me aside, behind a wave of kids who bang their way through.

'This isn't a joke, Stella. I don't know who you are, or what you are, but if you're even part fae, then it's your job to play by the rules. You don't tell a human about magic. And you don't let them see you when they stray into the forest.'

'So you *do* live in the forest!'

'Maybe,' he says, and his voice shakes.

'Why are you at school if you're fae?' I demand.

'Why not?' he says. 'Why shouldn't we?'

I don't have an answer for that; I'm way out of my depth here. He looks utterly furious and not at all friendly right now.

'Zara's my friend,' I say. 'Can't we trust her?'

'Just wait,' he says under his breath as we enter the room. 'Wait until you've seen what you're doing. Come with me after school. I'll show you, and we'll talk then.'

'And then I'll tell her.'

'Then you can decide.'

But my stomach is full of wiggling nerves, and lunch tastes dry and strange. I don't know how to look Zara in the eye when there are secrets between us. I tell her I've got a headache, and try to lose myself in the food, but Yanny's pastries are definitely unsatisfying today. They turn to dust in my mouth as soon as I bite into them, and I notice he barely touches them, preferring the red apples and buttered rye bread I brought, and Zara's tiny round cheese biscuits.

He doesn't show a sign that he's bothered about anything, and that only makes me worry more. If he's truly fae, and my Nan's books are accurate, he could probably hide just about anything and never let it show on his face.

11

I have to head out with Zara at the end of the day. She's been so sweet about my pretend headache all afternoon, I genuinely now feel a bit sick. I walk with her to the gate, and then she spots her mum waiting down the road.

'I'll see you tomorrow,' she says. 'Hope you feel better.'

'Thank you,' I manage, and I watch as she bolts down the road. I stand for a long while, watching her get into the car, watching it manoeuvre into the busy road, wondering what I'm doing. I came here for school. For humanity. For a friend like Zara. That's all I wanted. But I also want to know what's going on in Winterspell. I want to know what it means to be fae. And since I can't go in there, this is my chance.

I whip back in through the gate and race up the steps to the lobby before I can change my mind. Mrs Edge watches me crash through reception and shakes her head, but she says nothing. I head up the wide enchanted staircase to the first floor, and then on to some older, worn steps, where Yanny is waiting.

'Ready?' he asks.

'I don't know,' I say. 'I don't like lying to Zara.'

'If you weren't ready, you wouldn't be here,' he says.

And there doesn't really seem a good answer to that. I nod, and he whispers a word at the top of the steps, and the old wooden door swings open. On the other side, candles flare in sconces on the walls of a narrow corridor. It's cold up here, and draughty. It's like another school entirely. I pull my coat tight as Yanny walks on.

'What're we going to do?' I whisper. The candles gutter as we go, making shadows swoop and dance.

'Just have a look around so you know what you're missing. Don't worry – nobody's going to eat you!'

He grins, turning to me, but the grin is full of sharp teeth.

'Yanny!'

A man swoops down the corridor to us, cloak flying, his small round face creviced and pitted with scars.

'Ooh, a new student!' the man says, coming to a stop and peering at us with his head to one side.

'Ah, not really,' says Yanny, looking between us with

an awkward grimace of a smile. 'At least, she is new, but . . . I was just showing her around. Sorry. I didn't think you'd be here, sir.'

'And yet, here I am!' The man gleams. 'You have been caught out, Yanny.' He gives me a sharp look. 'Perhaps you had reason. Stella, is it?' he asks. 'I heard about your *trial* period. Mrs Edge was most curious about you.'

I open my mouth, but nothing comes out.

'She says she doesn't know much about fae magic,' Yanny says. 'But there's something there. So I thought . . .'

'Quite right,' the man says with a brisk nod. 'So, Stella – not a forest dweller, then?'

I shake my head, trying to calm the fizz in my blood. Whoever this man is, whatever this place is, there is power here. How are these worlds colliding? I thought the forest was magic, and that school would be . . . not magic. I stare into his unblinking gaze.

'But Yanny's right – there is *something*,' he says, tilting his head to the other side. 'How curious. Well, now you are here, so welcome. This is the Magical Department. I am Principal Ashworth. Come along – let's have a talk. Onward!'

He hustles down the corridor to a narrow, winding

staircase that takes us up into a round study with crinkled glass windows on every side.

'Now,' he says, perching on the edge of a broad wooden desk. 'Stella. You've seen our magical underbelly. You will have to sign the contract. Yanny generally has good instincts. Have you magic?'

'A little,' I say. 'Spell-work, charms – nothing very exciting.'

'And you are?'

I stare at him. 'Pardon?'

'What sort of a creature are you? There are humans with some magic. Are you one of those?'

I stare between him and Yanny. There's something searching and eager about both of them. If I told them the truth about my heritage – that the dreaded Shadow King is my father – what would they do to me? Nan always worried they might never accept me after all the misery he's caused.

'Ahh, yes. Human,' I say. 'We have lots of books. My nan says there is fae blood in our history . . .'

'I see,' says Principal Ashworth. 'Well, they say that we all have a little fae in us, somewhere. In some, it is more pronounced.' He fingers the tiny sharp horns that poke through his curling brown hair.

How did I miss those?

'And we may choose, sometimes, to hide the signs,' he says. 'So. Perhaps you are hiding; perhaps all that you possess is an instinct for our words. In any case, you must sign the contract.'

He produces a scroll from a small drawer in the front of the desk. It unspools, inch after inch of brown paper rushing to the floor, and he holds out an old ink pen with a wide brass nib crusted in black ink.

At least, I *hope* it's black ink. Right now, in this sun-flashed room, with this strange small man, and Yanny staring beside me, it could be almost anything.

'What is it?' I ask.

'Security contract,' says Principal Ashworth. 'Provides that you will neither take nor insert any magic from this place; that you will keep our secrets; that you will take all precautions when entering and exiting; reset the charms; respect the boundaries of your fellow magical students; work hard on your lessons . . .' He thrusts the pen at me. 'So, sign!'

'What if I accidentally let something slip?'

He takes back the pen. 'Are you prone to accidents?'

'No.'

'And you have some familiarity with the fae world.

With our words, and our spells. So, you already know how to keep such things safe.'

'Uh, yes. But. Can I tell my nan?'

'Is she human?'

'She's a ghost,' I say, my tongue already too tied from the unfamiliar lies.

They stare at me, and I shrug.

'How interesting!' Principal Ashworth nods. 'Then you may tell her. Besides, there are life-and-death provisos, should the need arise. Now sign, or I'll have to eject you, and there will be no coming back!'

I look at Yanny. 'You didn't say . . .'

'What are you worried about?' he asks, no help whatsoever. 'You already knew there was magic out there, and you knew to keep it a secret . . .'

'But magical contracts?' I hiss. 'Everyone knows they're a bad idea.'

'You're confusing your fae stories with your fairy stories,' says Principal Ashworth. 'We're not the Grimm brothers, and you aren't a little girl in a gingerbread house. Now, if you'd like to continue this little tour, you'll have to sign!'

He grins, and his teeth are a little pointed, but his eyes are warm, so I take a deep breath, pluck the pen from his outstretched hand, and sign the paper.

'Excellent,' he says, winding it back up again. 'You will join our lessons. Whatever affinity you have for our magic, we must explore it and work out what to do with you. There are rules – and customs – that you should know, whether you're human or fae, or something in between. Magic is not something to be taken lightly. Nor to be discussed downstairs in the regular lessons. Yanny will advise, if you need it. He is a *fairly* good student, and he has already asserted himself as your guide, so I will entrust you to his care.' He casts a glance at Yanny before turning back to me.

'Lessons start at 7.30 in the morning,' he continues, 'and finish by 8.45. And there's the odd differential, such as history and science, when you'll come to us. Welcome, Stella. I am sure you'll find what you need here, and perhaps a little more besides . . .'

He winks and flaps us out of the room, his cloak billowing.

I turn to Yanny at the top of the narrow steps, and he blows his cheeks out.

'You could have warned me,' I say, as he hustles me down and whisks us along the corridor to a circular, cavernous hall, where the ceiling rises in a spire, bookshelves winding up its sides. Shining wood ladders stretch right up through all the shelves, getting narrower as they go. The whole place sings at me and makes my head spin.

'The hall-slash-library,' he says.

'What have you got me into, Yanny?'

'What have I got *myself* into,' he retorts, not looking the slightest bit apologetic. He looks up at the rows of books, and his eyes flash with streaks of amber. 'Stupid. I should've left it all alone.' He looks back at me. 'I thought I could show you around without Ashworth finding us. I didn't mean to scare you.' He sighs, but there's still a glint in his eye as he leads me out.

'What kind of magic do you have?' I ask.

'Hmm?'

'You and Principal Ashworth – you both have the same kind of magic. Only, not the same . . .'

He turns back to me. 'How do you know we're not the same?'

'It just feels different.'

He frowns.

'You're very perceptive for someone who claims to have so little magic of their own.'

'We have books. Words. I know the old legends.'

'Ah well, then you should know what I am,' he says.

And he marches off again.

I watch him go, registering the lightness of his tread, the length of his limbs, the way his shadow on the wall is not quite a true reflection. It flickers at the edges, dancing and shifting as he moves.

'Well, you're not a centaur,' I say, catching up with him. 'Are you?'

'I'm a fairy,' he says. 'And you're taking all the fun out of this.' He scratches at the back of his neck. 'We should have done this in the morning. . . I need to get home.'

'I thought fairies were smaller.'

'That's because you've only seen pictures in books. Are we supposed to wear bluebells on our heads too, as hats?'

I try to hide a smile; he looks very cross about it.

'No . . . but I thought you had wings.'

He winces and keeps on moving.

'So –' he indicates a darkened room on the right of the corridor, empty and lit only by a red-filtered lantern swinging from the ceiling – 'this is history. Lessons are on Mondays, after last bell.'

'OK,' I say, drawing my timetable out of my bag and

grabbing one of my new sparkly pens to make a note of it.

He rolls his eyes and moves on again. 'Next is earth science. Trees, water, elements, the natural world.'

'Does that mean things like mer-fae . . . and dryads?'

'Your books are getting old,' he says, and there's a shiver in his voice.

'Yanny?'

'What is it?'

'You're angry. I'm sorry if I'm not saying the right things . . .'

'Dryads are mostly in hiding these days, and nobody has seen a mer-fae for years. Your books clearly don't cover recent history. Let's just get this done.'

He flits up the rest of the corridor. There's a room for fae ethics and practical magic, glamouring and bewitching; and another, where the walls glow in soft amber shades, and low chairs are arranged in small huddles.

'What's this for? Why is it so dark up here?'

'No electricity,' he says. 'It doesn't work well around magic. This is time-out. Most of the fae kids are glamouring while they're downstairs, and it gets hard.' His voice sounds strained.

'What's wrong?'

'I'm fine,' he says. He looks at me, gives a shadow of a bleak, sharp smile. 'I just need to get home.'

'What's it like, in Winterspell?' I ask carefully. 'Are the stories about the shadows true?'

His face tightens, and I immediately regret asking.

'I don't know about stories,' he says. 'The shadows are real.' He winces, arching his back. 'And I'm not talking about that now.'

'Sorry – I just wondered . . .' I frown, as his eyes flash amber again. 'Does it hurt, to glamour? You don't need to do it in front of me. I'm all signed up now, remember?'

'It isn't about you,' he hisses. 'I need to get through the school, and town, and home.'

'Should we sit here for a moment, then? It's safe here, isn't it?'

His shadow writhes behind him, and there's a dark flash of tattered shadowy wings.

'I can't,' he says. 'Got to get back. I should've done this another day . . .'

'I'll come with you.'

We rush through the corridors, down the shining steps, and he is a bright force beside me, static like a silver needle pricks through the air between us.

'How many magical kids are here?' I ask, as we get out of the front gate.

'Thirteen.' He grins. 'Lucky to have you, makes fourteen.'

'Thirteen is lucky in some cultures,' I say, making my voice bright and chatty. 'In China, and the—'

'Not in ours,' he cuts me off.

'That's why you wanted me to start lessons?'

'Partly,' he says. 'Also, because you have magic. I can feel it, and so can you.'

'I don't know about that,' I huff, as we dash through the streets, and the lights of the shops make the pavements shine beneath the pale mist of rain. Our footsteps are quick and light, and Yanny is panicking, I can feel it. We cross the road by the bakery, and he stumbles on the kerb.

'I've got to run,' he says. 'I'll see you tomorrow – 7.30. Ashworth does assembly on Thursdays. The others will be there.'

'OK.'

'Sorry,' he whispers. 'Grumpy.'

'It's OK. See you tomorrow.'

He nods, and the air around him vibrates. Then he's gone, fleet-footed, darting between cars and away towards the forest.

I stand there in the rain for a moment, my feet are numb, my hands prickle.

There were wings. Flimsy things that curled over his shoulders, broader than his back, but hardly more than shadows. I saw them unfurl and snag at the air. Saw the way they fluttered as he fled, with nothing more than an echo of movement.

What happened to his wings?

The Fairy

One of the boldest, most mischievous of the fae, the fairy is large in number and of earth, and air, and water, and fire. They tend to have large families, and some would say more courage than sense. It is they who defend the fae realm, and they who play tricks on passing humans. They are the ones most frequently spotted, but they are very good at glamouring, which means they may easily hide or change their appearance.

There is tell of earth fairies who live in the human world *as humans*, using their magic to round their ears and veil their wings. Hiding magic, though, is no mean feat, and fairies are prone to sickness. Their bodies are fragile in the world of men.

FIGHT – 7

FLIGHT – 10

MAGIC – 8

DISGUISE – 10

12

It's getting dark as I reach home, the forest is more shadowed than ever. I skirt the house and linger on the moors by the river for a while, knowing Nan and Peg will be full of questions about my day, and not having a clue how I can answer them truthfully.

As I watch, I spot movement between the trees. Something small and bright bursts out and races fast as lightning towards me. I squeal, staggering back as it bounds up to my chest, all sharp claws and static and . . . soft fur. A small, vaguely triangular face looks up at mine, claws latched firmly into my coat, green eyes flashing.

It's a cat!

What kind of a cat bounces out of the forest like that?

'Hi,' I say, reaching out and untangling it from my coat, holding it at arm's length. It's a tiny little tabby, its fur striped in shades of white and silver-grey flecks glinting in the darkening light. 'Who are you?'

It doesn't answer; it just stares at me. I put it down on the cold grass, and it walks around my ankles, before sitting on my left boot.

'Oh!'

Then another wild creature bursts out from the direction of the house and whizzes to my shoulder. Peg, being a bird.

'Look, Peg,' I say. 'It's a cat!'

'Is it though?' he demands, his golden beak snapping by my ear as he peers down.

I pick up the cat. It nestles into my arms and starts to purr.

'Seems like it to me,' I say. 'Maybe it strayed into the forest by mistake, and that's why it bolted out so quickly.'

'Hmmm.'

'Nan will know,' I say.

And so we head to the house: me and a small, trembling tabby cat, and one rather cross bird-imp.

It'll be a good distraction from school news, anyway.

'I'm dreadfully allergic to cats,' says Nan, perching on the edge of her blue chair, her lower legs and feet only vaguely visible.

'Nan.' I stare at her.

The cat is sleeping in my lap, and Peg sits on the mantelpiece, his tail swinging over the flames.

'*What?* I am!'

'I really don't think ghosts can be allergic to animals.' She frowns.

'Well, *I* might be. I'm not your ordinary sort of ghost, you know.' She narrows her eyes. 'Did you bring her back to distract us from news of school?'

'No!'

'So,' she says. 'Tell me about your day. Don't leave anything out.'

'It was pretty normal . . .'

'No such thing. Come on – out with it.'

'The lunch was good. And I like maths. Zara is really nice. She's new too. Her mum moved them here a little while ago . . .'

And there's a whole floor full of magic, where the fae learn their history. And I lied. I lied, and I said I was human, and Yanny's eyes knew that I was lying, but what could I say: 'I am the child of the fae king who cursed your home'?

'Zara?' Nan leans forward. 'Who is Zara?'

'A girl at school!'

'Human?'

'Yes, Nan. Of course.' I hold my breath, hoping she doesn't ask any more about that. I've never lied outright to her face; I'm not sure I could. And I know she isn't going to be happy about me being in a school with the fae she's spent so long trying to keep me away from.

'*Bright*, "Zara" means,' she says. '*Bright and shining*, I think.'

'It suits her.' I smile, looking down at the cat. It's very small; perhaps even just a kitten still. I always wanted a pet.

'This little cat must go,' says Peg, shaking his head, twin plumes of steam escaping his nostrils.

The kitten opens one green eye and stares at him.

'You said she came out of Winterspell.' Peg's brow furrows. 'Who knows what she might be.'

'She's a cat, and I'm keeping her. She can be my familiar – like Peg is yours, Nan.'

They huff together.

'How do you know it's a she?' Peg demands. 'Something magical? I mean, if it's going to be a familiar, it needs to be a *bit* magical. Can't just have any old cat being a familiar.'

'You just said that she was probably a monster! Now she's any old cat?'

'She is an unknown, to be treated with caution,' says Nan.

'Fine. I won't tell her all our secrets. Yet. But she is staying.'

'Well aren't you growing up quickly with all your new attitudes?' she says drily. 'What are you going to call this *pet* of yours, then?'

'Teacake!' I blurt.

Peg puts his horned head in his hands, and Nan opens her mouth and snaps it shut again. Teacake's purr rumbles through me.

'Really?' Peg asks, raising his head and staring at me. 'You do know that a familiar is an important creature? That if it's true, your bond will be unassailable, that she will be by your side until the day you die – or even after.' He gives Nan a look. 'That she will be your champion when you need one, your adviser, your closest ally, your most magical weapon in times of need? That she will sacrifice everything to be with you, that your care for her must be foremost in your mind, no matter what comes your way?'

'Yes, Peg.' I meet his eye. 'I know what a familiar is. It's one of the only things I really do know for sure. Do you think you haven't taught me that?'

'She's probably just a lost kitty, and she'll be gone back home within a week,' Nan says. 'For all your melodrama, the pair of you, let's not get carried away. She looks fairly ordinary to me.'

I bury my fingers in Teacake's thick fur and tickle her neck. She rolls over in my lap, showing us all her pale belly, and gives a little chirrup, staring at Peg and flexing her claws. The flames roar in the fireplace, and Peg's tail makes sparks as it swishes, and Nan settles back into her chair, her eyes dancing as she watches.

I think she likes Teacake, really.

The Sprite

Ahh, lucky is the soul blessed by the sprite. They are few and far between, and their power is vast, for it is the power of trees, and rivers, and mountains, and of the moon itself. Nimble, stalk-limbed, they might even pass for human, were it not for the verdant hues of their hair and the tiny horns that sometimes grow from their upper brow.

Peaceful, they may be – but ware, fisherman, to ask for permission before you plunder a water sprite's river. And ware, woodcutters, for the wood sprite's rage is as vast as all of Winterspell, if harm should come to its dearest. A wood sprite who has lost its tree is a terrible, howling creature. A monster made, indeed.

FIGHT – 8

FLIGHT – 10

MAGIC – 8

DISGUISE – 10

13

It's dark when I leave for school, and the ground is winter hard. My breath steams against the brittle cold air. Teacake follows me all the way down the lane to the river and when I look back the house is just visible, lights glimmering in the windows, frost sweeping down over the roof. I reach down and give her a fuss and tell her to head home. Green eyes linger on mine, and then she turns and starts to head back.

'Good girl,' I whisper with a smile, watching her go. She's a tiny bright figure trotting down past the unruly hedgerows. I wonder where she did come from. As I stand there watching, I can just make out the call of the centauride, deep in the woods. Winterspell is a dark sweep up Cloudfell Mountain from here, a chill mist gathered about the lower reaches, and folds of new snow at its peak.

Teacake stops dead, her ears pricked. And the dawn

chorus begins with a clamour. I take a deep breath and turn my back on all of it, heading into school, and up the stairs, through the charms to the hall in the round tower for my first magical assembly.

Principal Ashworth is like a cricket at the front of the room, constantly moving, his fingers fiddling with the edge of his cloak. I scoot in, find Yanny, and take a seat in the rickety wood chair next to him. Round windows look out to a still pink sky, and the metalwork on the spines of all the books in the twisting vaults of the tower gleams.

'Morning,' I whisper.

I'm shaky with nerves; it feels like the first day all over again. There are about a dozen kids in here, and most of them are looking at me. I smile, and a couple smile back. Others definitely don't look as friendly.

'Drop your glamours, if you're still wearing them,' Principal Ashworth says. 'Save your energy. You are among friends!' He beams.

'How do we know that?' asks one girl sitting towards the back of the room, looking at me with a scowl on her face. Her dark hair is piled up on top of her head, held there with what look like ice-blue knitting needles.

'Because you put your trust in me, and I have kept

your safety for generations,' snaps Principal Ashworth. 'A little scepticism can be forgiven. But a lack of manners, Tash – that is an ugly thing indeed.'

She folds her arms and slouches down in her chair, letting her glamour slip. Her features change by infinite degrees, so that her eyes are silver, with narrow, cat-like pupils, and her hair is roped like fine looping vines around the needles. She glares at me as I watch and bares her teeth at me; they are steel-bright and dagger-sharp. I turn back to the front of the room, trying to repress a shudder.

'Don't mind her,' Yanny says. 'She's always grumpy in the mornings. Moon sprites don't like daylight.'

'She's pretty fierce,' I reply, stealing another glance and wondering if I'd look anything like she does without Nan's glamour.

There are so many fae here, it's a bit like a dream, or like one of Nan's stories got tied up with one of my favourite books about human schools. There are some who look a little like Yanny – perhaps fairies too – and there's a girl who looks like she could be Tash's cousin. There's a boy with a greenish tint to his skin and hair like dark moss, and a couple of others who seem entirely human, save for their pointed ears and shadow wings, and a girl with golden skin and the same tiny horns as Principal Ashworth. A couple of adults, who I guess must be teachers, sit to one side looking faintly bored. One has the same neat, twisted horns; the other is grey-skinned and stocky, with curling silver hair and the most beautiful dark lacy wings. He catches me looking and winks.

'That's Mr Flint,' Yanny whispers. 'And that's Miss Fern. She's a sprite—'

'Our new girl here is Stella Brigg,' Principal Ashworth booms over him, gesturing at me with an outflung arm. 'Welcome, Stella. We are excited to have you with us.' He grins, and the whole room is silent as everybody turns to stare at me.

'What sort of a fae is Stella?' asks Tash, her voice all innocence and curiosity. 'Might we be permitted to know?'

Principal Ashworth glares at her, but it's clear everybody wants to hear my answer. What am I going to say?

'I'm not fae,' I whisper eventually.

'Stella hasn't worked that out yet,' Principal Ashworth says. 'Our lives are not all so simple – so cut and dried. Stella has some magic, or she would not be here. That is enough for me, and it will be enough for all of you.'

He pivots on one heel and makes for a whiteboard in the corner of the room, where a new timetable has been drawn in wavering lines, and gets everybody to copy down the revisions while he talks about Mrs Ingot, who will be joining the school next week to cover Ms Spicer's maternity leave. It's a lot like an assembly downstairs, to be honest, only there's the odd warning about glamours easily slipping during PE, and about the spell room, which must not be used without a teacher present.

'Finally,' says Principal Ashworth, 'end of term is coming up, and I'm sure you're looking forward to some well-earned rest. Be warned, there will be homework – you must not let all the work you've been doing go to waste over the break!'

'How can you stand keeping secrets from Zara like this?' I whisper at Yanny as we head back upstairs to history later on. Zara was definitely suspicious earlier, when we'd clattered in late together after the assembly, and I can't help feeling it's only going to get worse. 'It's making me feel horrible.'

'It's just necessary,' he says. 'It's not against her; it's just not anything to do with her either. Some humans have magic – *you* know that, apparently. If she has any in her, she hasn't worked it out yet. Most people never do.'

Miss Capaldi is the languages and history teacher. She has pale, wiry hair that spirals down over narrow shoulders, and silver eyes that flash, and she welcomes me with a hungry grin that sends jagged splinters down my spine.

'New blood, I see,' she hisses, tilting her head as she studies me. 'Have you all met Stella Brigg, my dears?' She glances around at the rest of the class. Everybody is here – all staring, as usual. 'Isn't she quite the enigma? Neither fae nor fully human . . . And what a name! A star *and* a bridge. What do you bridge, little star?'

If I ever knew words, I do not know them now. They have left me entirely. I barely remember how to breathe.

'Well, we shall see,' she says, releasing me from her stare. I stumble to the nearest seat and fall into it, ignoring Yanny and everybody else. My heart is thumping like a drum through my body. 'For now, our studies turn to darker things than stars, my dears.'

Miss Capaldi turns to the blank wall at one end

of the room and raises an arm. A map of what I suppose must be Winterspell rolls out across the white space.

'We come to the place where few stars now shine. You have all heard of our generations of peace under the Cloudfell Mountain. That was before the Shadow King; before the stag came upon us and brought ruin in his wake. Who can tell me how such a thing occurred?'

Nobody stirs.

'No,' she says. 'I don't suppose you want to. However, we must. Through history, we learn. Through mistakes. What were the mistakes?'

'They thought they were safe!' Tash calls out from somewhere behind me.

'Yes. Under the king and queen, they thought they were safe, all those fae folk. They knew that danger may come from humanity, and so that is where they fixed their eyes. The danger came from the wilderness itself. From the Shadow King, fae through and through. Our own king, torn asunder by sickness and grief. Who hides in the cursed palace that none can find, and who has blighted our own Winterspell with shadows, thick and fast as the cruellest beast. And so we fight, especially in the night, when they obscure the moon and all the stars. The days are hard; the nights are harder. That is why your parents take such care. Why so many of them spend their nights out in Winterspell. Sometimes we win, and sometimes we lose. But you already know that much . . .'

She is quiet for a moment, and the class is silent before her. Yanny's eyes are lowered, his hands clasped tight on the desk. Sorrow shudders through the room and makes my eyes sting.

Why did I not know how bad things were?

'And so. To legends!' Miss Capaldi turns the mood with the bright silver of her voice. 'Remind us, Yanny.'

'The Lost Prince.'

Yanny says it quietly, but it sends a rush of energy through the room, and his voice is echoed by all the others. It isn't just a name, or an idea; it's a bolt of iron, welded to them with absolute certainty. Miss Capaldi nods, her eyes glinting.

'His arrival will herald the change we need. Some doubt he exists – and who knows the truth of it? Legends were ever vague and quite often completely wrong. Some say he is the one who will find the palace and challenge the Shadow King. In the meantime, it is our job to live. To fight and to keep our homes and our children – you – safe. To prepare for our futures, no matter where they might lie. And so, children, we will today be looking at the history of tree preservation, our most important role.'

She stares about the room. I slide low in my chair as the map on the wall redraws itself so that we are now looking at the swaying forms of bright oaks and willow trees.

Who is the Lost Prince?

I have a horrible, terrible feeling that it might refer to me.

Is that why Nan was so keen to keep me away from everybody? Because she knows they're waiting for some fictional child who definitely isn't me? I breathe through a wave of panic, relieved when Miss Capaldi turns to the illustrations on the wall and begins a fierce lecture on the patterns and preservation of the oldest trees in the woods.

There's a strange silence between her words, and the light filters through old windows almost like mist. There is no sniggering, no shuffling or whispering – just her warrior voice blooming through us all, speaking of the greatest bonds between trees and ancient heroes. I watch as the scenes come to life on the wall by her side, as she twists from the images to us, her hands spread, her eyes flashing.

I need to know about that legend.

'Nan!' I clatter into the kitchen, and she blooms through the fireplace, bright eyed. Teacake is perched on the hearth by the embers of this morning's fire, and Peg is swinging from the copper chandelier, eating tiny fish from a little porcelain dish.

'Yes, dear?'

'What is this about a Lost Prince?'

Peg chokes on his fish, and the dish crashes down towards the table. Nan catches it, and then settles herself at the table, gesturing for me to join her.

'Haven't you worked that out?' she asks.

'But you've never told me anything about it!'

'I needed to hide you,' she says. 'From your father, and from the shadows. From all of the fae, for goodness knows none of them can keep a secret. So I hid us here, and I glamoured us all . . . and I left behind me the legend of the Lost Prince. So that they would know we had not forgotten them, and so that if they should ever catch a glimpse of a small brown-haired *girl* playing near the forest, should my glamour fail for even a moment, they would not suspect. You are the Lost Prince they speak of. But –' her eyes narrow – 'how do you know about this, Estelle?'

'It was just . . . something I picked up.' I wince, realizing too late that I've given myself away. She only calls me Estelle when I've done something wrong.

'Pardon?'

'There's lots of talk about Winterspell at school,' I say. 'I mean, there's bound to be. It's right on the doorstep of the village, and they think it's haunted. The kids talk about the strange lights, and the sounds of battle . . . How they have to avoid the whole place. And the legend of the Lost Prince . . .'

Peg glowers, but he doesn't say anything, and Nan seems to be satisfied with my rushed explanation.

'People talk.' She nods. 'And so close to Winterspell, there has always been fae blood in the village. People with a little magic, a little faith in what they can't see – like Mrs Mandrake. I suppose it's no surprise the children would have heard the legend.'

'Lost Prince,' I say, looking down at myself. 'Oh, Nan.'

'You'll see.' She smiles. 'Just give it time, my love.'

But she obviously doesn't know how bad it is in there

for the fae. She's been away so long, she doesn't know they send their children out to a human school just to give them a chance of a future. She's spun them a lie about a Lost Prince, but he'll never come for them. I don't have that kind of magic, that kind of power.

I don't belong in there at all.

14

The week rushes past in a tumble of falling autumn leaves, bitter frosty mornings, and the dash from lesson to lesson, from magic to non-magic, from ancient legends to the tinkle of glass beakers in science lessons. By Thursday morning, my head is buzzing. Assembly is fraught with tension after another bad night in the forest, and Tash is looking more venomous by the day. Yanny stays close, but he looks troubled, and I cannot keep this up.

Of course I can't. Ever since I heard of Nan's ridiculous legend, it's been haunting me. How can I let them wait for something that doesn't exist? That will never come to pass?

'What's going on with you?' Yanny asks as we scramble up from our seats after a grim-faced lecture from Principal Ashworth about staying out of the forest canopy. The gathering winter, he told us, has made it more brittle than ever, and shadows are waiting to catch those who fall. Playing up in the higher branches, we were warned, is strictly forbidden. 'I know this stuff might not seem important to you, but you should know it anyway. If you're ever in Winterspell, it could save your life. Did you even hear a word of what he said?'

'Of course!' I say. 'I was just . . . I was distracted. Sorry.' I take a deep breath while Yanny stares at me. 'I need to tell you something.'

'OK,' he says. 'But not here.'

He pauses at the door by the charms to settle his glamour over himself. It's a bit of a struggle, by the look of it. Tash glares at me, and he turns to talk to her in a lowered tone that sounds part angry, part reassuring.

'Later, then,' I say, leaving them to it, feeling guilty. I can see how it strains them all to hide their best, most magical features.

Would people really be that horrified if they saw Yanny for who he really is? Or me, for that matter? What is the difference in me? What am I, underneath Nan's glamour? I'm starting to wonder if I'm the monster my father is. Why have I let this carry on? Why didn't I tell Yanny right from the start?

Because I was afraid.

I dig my nails into my palms and swear to myself that I won't waste another moment, but Zara is hovering when I get downstairs, and she spots me as soon as my feet land on the shining wood floor.

'Hey,' I say.

'Stella!' she says. 'There you are. Did you get past me? I've been here for ages!'

'I didn't see you. I got swept in the tide.'

She seems to accept it easily enough, and we head off to tutorial, and for a while, I think I'm going to get away with it. But Zara is no fool. And Yanny knows now that I've got something to tell him, so his eyes blaze every time he looks at me.

By lunchtime, it's clear to Zara that something is going on, and I don't know how to steer us all back in the right direction.

'What?' she demands, once Yanny is done hoovering up all our food. 'What's up with you two?'

'Nothing,' I say, focusing on very neatly refolding the wax paper I'd wrapped my sandwiches in.

Zara scowls at us and folds her arms.

'It's fine,' Yanny says through a yawn. 'My mum knows Stella's nan, and she's invited them both for tea tonight. And Stella's just worried that you'll feel left out.'

'Oh!' says Zara. 'How weird that they knew each other all along! Did you know, Stella?'

'No!' I squeak.

'Well of course I don't mind,' she says, looking between us with a smile that doesn't quite reach her eyes. She packs up her lunchbox, taking a really long time to file away all the little pots. 'Maybe we could all do tea together another time?'

'Yes,' I say, relief coursing through me as her face brightens. 'Come to mine next week. I'll check it out with Nan, but I know she's really keen to meet you.'

It should be OK. As long as Peg stays a bird, and Nan stays in her chair . . .

After school, I head back towards home with Yanny. Zara waved us off cheerfully enough, and we live in the same direction, so the lie looks true enough. I've promised to talk to him, but the words won't come, and the further we go, the harder it gets, until even my footsteps are clumsy, and the space between us is full of tension.

'Are you waiting for a written invitation?' he bursts out eventually, as we reach the lane by my house. His eyes are brighter, his hair glints with gold strands, and the shadow wings are just about visible against the darkening day.

'What? No!'

'Then tell me. Tell me what you are, Stella. I knew from the very start that you were *something*. I tried to tell myself I was wrong – but I wasn't, was I?'

I take a deep breath. Finger the acorn at my throat.

'I'm sorry,' I whisper.

'For what?' he demands.

'For lying to you. I wanted to make friends, and I didn't know when I started at the school that you'd be there. That fae would be there. I just wanted . . . I wanted to meet people . . .'

'So you *are* fae?'

'Yes. No. I . . . Yes. I'm a sprite.'

'So why do you live out here? Why don't you live in Winterspell?'

'My nan took me in, when my mother died. She raised me here, to keep me safe from the shadows. The house was built by her grandfather – he was a human. And Nan glamoured me when we fled. She used the last of her magic to do it, and it's stuck. I don't even know what I truly look like!'

'If only we all had enchanted houses to hide in,' he says, his eyes flicking up at the red brick house and the smoke curling from its chimney.

'I'm sorry.'

He shrugs. 'You may as well come back,' he says, registering the charms on the silver wire fence around the house. 'If you want to. Aren't you curious about your true home?'

'Ye-ess . . . but what about the shadows?'

'The shadows I fight every day?' He shrugs. 'You'll survive them.'

I stare at him, and then Peg comes wheeling over, landing on my shoulder and staring fiercely at Yanny. Of course, he can't say anything, because he's pretending to be a normal never-before-seen breed of bird, but his claws dig into my shoulder like curving question marks, and I've had enough of deceptions for the day.

'Yanny, this is Peg,' I say, as Yanny watches intently. 'Peg, this is Yanny. He's a fairy.'

'Well I guessed that much,' says Peg, as Yanny's eyes widen. 'What sort of a fairy is he?'

'Um . . .'

Peg glares at Yanny.

'I'm a fire fairy,' Yanny says. 'And . . . what sort of a bird are you?'

'Ha!' caws Peg. 'You think I'm a bird!'

'I think you're parading as a bird,' Yanny says. 'It seemed rude to ask what sort of imp you are.'

Peg mutters something under his breath and then sighs as Teacake charges up to us, winding around my ankles with a yowling sort of purr.

'And who is this?' Yanny smiles, crouching.

'I call her Teacake.'

He gives me a quizzical look, tickling Teacake behind her ears. She scooches in close and gazes at him adoringly, her green eyes flickering like cold fire.

'It seemed to fit, at the time,' I say.

'I think it's fitting; she's got about as much brain as a teacake,' Peg says. 'Caught her attacking her own tail earlier and looking surprised when it hurt.'

I sigh. 'She's a kitten, Peg. Playing.'

He mutters again, and I wonder if Nan is about to join us at the gate, just to make this whole experience fully surreal, but as I stare towards the house, Peg announces that she's resting. Mrs Mandrake called in earlier with some more bits for me and tired her out. We're on our own for tea.

'Ah, actually,' I say, watching as Teacake licks Yanny's hand and makes him laugh. The sky is leaden over our heads and our house looks cold; he's the brightest thing for miles. 'I'm going to go to Yanny's for tea.'

'In the forest?' Peg demands, lifting from my shoulder and hovering in my face, golden eyes sparking.

'Yes.'

'But, Stella! Nan wouldn't like that!'

'I won't be late,' I tell him, reaching out and cupping him in my hands. 'Promise, Peg, dear.' I lean in and kiss him.

'I forbid you to go in,' he says.

'Peg! If you're that worried, you should come too . . .'

'Ah, no. I can't. I told you – I'm not allowed in there now.'

I stare at him. 'You didn't say you weren't *allowed*! Why?'

'I'll tell you –' he sighs – 'inside!'

'Later, when I'm back,' I say, steeling myself and setting off before he can say anything else.

I'm tired of his secrets. The sun is low in the sky, and shadows stretch across the golden plain, and when I dare to look back, he's watching us, a darting, whirling thing among the brambles. Why can't he come with us into the forest? I should have stayed and found out. I hesitate, full of guilt and tangled feelings, but Yanny walks on, and Teacake looks up at me with a questioning chirrup.

'I'm going in,' I whisper, steeling myself. 'I need to, Teacake. You understand?'

She sits down and winds her smoky tail neatly over her front paws.

I sigh.

Yanny reaches the edge of the forest and turns, raising one eyebrow as if in challenge, as the shadows cluster behind him. It's only tea with a friend, for goodness sake. Most kids do that all the time. I blow a kiss at Teacake and walk to Yanny, to the forest.

'OK?' he asks. His shoulders are set and stiff, his face drawn. 'You don't have to come in. I shouldn't have pressured you.'

'It's fine,' I manage.

If he can do this every day, I can do it too. They're only shadows after all.

Nightfall

In the deepest dark of day, and in the starless night, there he shall be. Noble – once – and full of pride: the Stag who is the Shadow King.

He treads light upon the roots of Winterspell, and he fears nothing, for he has nothing. The shadows who surround him are his subjects, and they are borne of his own misery and malice. He surrounds himself with them for he cannot bear the light. The Stag is lonely, an angry figure of loss, but his power is dark as the antlers that twist over his brow, and so destruction follows in his wake and spreads from his every touch.

The trees of Winterspell grieve to see him, and the fae of the forest fight. They fight with all that they are, and they hope for the Lost Prince, whose arrival will change everything.

15

The grass gets deeper as we go, and the sound of the place fills my mind. It's a whispering song, of autumn leaves drifting, of streams rushing over rocks, of starlight through a canopy of winter branches. Yanny's feet are silent over a carpet of leaves and soft bracken, and I try to tread as carefully as he does as we enter the dark heart of the forest, but every move I make feels clumsy and distorted, as if I'm walking for the first time. The shadows flutter at the edge of my vision, and there's a strange vibration through the air that doesn't seem to bother Yanny.

'Steady!' he says, as I trip over the outstretched root of a towering oak with a glittering golden trunk. He catches my arm and stops me from falling.

'Sorry!'

He shrugs. 'I've spent all my life here; you haven't. Keep to the path – look.'

And there it is: a narrow spiral of harder ground leading further into the shadows, bordered by tiny ghost-pale flowers that swing their heads in my direction. Their voices are like chiming bells, but there are shadows that call louder. Between the trees and shuffling in the wind, they flit, in dark spaces, and the further in we go, the faster they get through the trees, just out of reach and almost out of sight, filling the air with darkness.

'OK?' Yanny asks, looking back.

'Don't worry about me,' I say, training my eyes on the path.

'That might be easier if you could stay on your feet!' he says with a surprised curse as I slip on some black ice and career into him, sending us crashing into the low-hanging, spiky branches of a nearby bush.

'So . . . sorry!' I manage, trying to repress sudden giggles that are mostly jangling nerves.

He grins, his teeth sharp, even as his eyes flick to the patches of darkness between the trees. And then there's a shuddering bellow from somewhere in the deep.

'No,' breathes Yanny. 'That's the Stag. We need to run.'

But the roots writhe beneath our feet, and the ivy that clings to the trees is a wild, snaring thing, and even Yanny is less sure-footed now. Ice gathers in sharp splinters on the path, and we slip and slide as we head further into the darkness. He grabs my hand as the ground around us begins to rumble, as the shadows clamour closer to the path. They are alive, gathered into the shapes of wild creatures, and they open their yawning mouths wide.

I should have stayed away.

'Here!' Yanny shouts, diving down beneath the reaching branches of a willow, fumbling with the latch of a trapdoor.

Golden light spills out. Voices – and the smell of food.

'Come on!' he says, breathing hard. 'Why are they so crazed about you – get in here!'

But something's making it hard to move forward. Something reaching, grasping. Something that cries through the trees and stampedes over the ground. A rush, coming harder and closer, that pulls at me and makes my eyes sting.

'Stella!' Yanny pulls me through the hatch, panic in his eyes, and the trapdoor slams shut over my head as he rushes me down shallow steps that have been cut into the earth.

'I'm sorry,' I say, recovering myself.

We're in a small, rounded hallway lit with veins of quartz, a corridor leading off in one direction. Tiny flowers nestle in the fine cracks, and ivy trails along the earth floor.

'They were so strong, Yanny . . . Did I make them worse?'

'I don't know about worse,' he whispers, looking from me back up to the hatch. He takes a deep breath and smiles, though he still looks a bit freaked out to me. 'We're here, now. Forget about it. Come and meet the others.'

He leads me down the corridor, past little alcoves where stacks of books and coppery pine cones nestle, and the quartz in the dark walls gets brighter as we go, until we arrive at a door that opens into a kitchen area. At one end, round windows look out on to the glittering stream. Heavy iron pans flash in the light of the glowing veins that criss-cross the ceiling, and beneath the windows, a long wooden table is laden with steaming copper dishes of knobbly potatoes and long-stemmed brown mushrooms, pale fish and sprouting green vegetables.

'Where is everybody?' I whisper.

Yanny grins. 'You can't see them?'

'Should I?' I ask, straining my eyes.

Here and there, a flash of movement, a swish of light. Then I hear a tiny, bright giggle, a spoon dances and falls to the floor – and there they are. A whole flock of near-Yannies staring at me from the benches that line the table, wide smiles mirroring his own.

'They were practising their glamouring,' Yanny whispers. 'Stella, meet my brothers, Fin, Dart and Ro – and my sister, Willow . . .'

Four small, freckled faces look up at me, and tiny hands shove at each other as they all squiggle together on the bench beneath the window.

'Fin is six; Dart and Ro are five; and Willow is four.'

I give them a smile, noting the whisper of wings at their backs. And then a woman with the same chestnut hair woven into elaborate braids charges in from the back of the house. She startles as she sees me standing there with Yanny, but recovers quickly, walking over and raising her hands to cup Yanny's face. Her cheeks are bright, her smile warm, but her eyes are troubled. Her own wings are faded, folded like lace at her back.

'Home,' she says. 'My lovely boy. I was worried, you didn't take your faelight, and the nights are drawing in.

Who have you brought with you?' She turns to me.

'This is Stella,' he says. 'She's new to the school. She lives outside the forest with her nan. So I thought I'd show her what she's missing . . . Stella, this is my mother, Elowen.'

'Ah!' She fixes her eyes on me, and the smile meets her eyes. 'Welcome, Stella. It is good to meet one of Yanny's school friends. Take a seat, both of you. I'm afraid it's fish again, and there is no butter, but I have a little rosemary and some oil . . .' She rummages in one of the cupboards as Yanny and I settle in beside one of his brothers on the bench facing the river, and takes out a dark, round loaf of bread, clattering it on to a board.

'What about Pa?' Yanny asks.

'Resting,' Elowen says. 'He had a tricky night last night.'

'What happened?'

'Oh, the usual,' she says, making her voice bright as she dishes food on to plates. 'Not for worrying now, Yanny. Eat your food. Rest. Your day has been just as full as anybody else's.'

He visibly unwinds at her words, and I realize there was just a touch of magic in them. The light in the room changes as we start to eat and fills all the corners, becoming a rosy glow that takes the edge off the lines on Elowen's face. Fin and Ro get into a bicker about who caught the best fish, and Willow stares at me while Elowen tries to feed her vegetables.

Yanny is quiet beside me, and when I look at him, I realize the glamour is fading. His eyes are brighter, his features sharper, and the magic that comes off him is wilder than ever. He flashes me a fierce grin, winking, and my throat is suddenly tight. It's so warm here, so noisy – so full of *life*. It's just how I imagined a big family might be, and even with the tension bubbling underneath, it still feels like a good place. Like home.

Would my family have been like this if my parents were still here? Would there have been this tide of chatter, this easy rest of a hand on a shoulder, of outrage turning so quickly to laughter? Would I have had brothers and sisters had the Plaga not struck? . . .

I force myself to eat while I watch them, and then there's a clatter and a shout that breaks through all the peace and makes the veins in the walls flicker with red.

Elowen puts a restraining hand on Yanny's arm as he darts up from the table.

'No. You have company. I'll go.'

'But you've been here with him all day.'

'It's fine, Yanny.'

'No,' he says. 'Stella wants to know all about the fae; she doesn't need to be sheltered. I'll go.'

He rushes up the corridor, and Elowen stares at her plate for a long moment before fixing her eyes on me. 'His pa is a bit under the weather. He works nights, and Winterspell isn't an easy place for fae at the moment, especially when the sun has set. You live outside?'

I nod.

'Good,' she says. 'You're a sprite – I can see it in you, though it is faint!'

'It's a glamour,' I say. 'My . . . my nan did it, and it's quite strong.'

'Isn't it,' she agrees, studying me.

She looks like she wants to say more, but then Yanny comes back in, an older version of himself following in his wake. The similarity is uncanny, and it sends a pang through me; his father is so thin and worn, his wings, like Elowen's, faded and tucked away.

'My pa, Fen. This is Stella.'

Fen smiles. 'Welcome, Stella. That's some name you have there.'

'Is it?' asks Ro.

134

'Stella means *star*. We could do with some more of those around here . . .'

'I'm not sure I'm that useful, really,' I say, and Elowen laughs, and the glow returns to the room as Fen takes his seat and praises his kids for the fish they caught while he slept.

Willow scooches up close to him, and he eats with one arm around her, but the weariness doesn't quite leave his eyes, and Yanny never visibly relaxes. He doesn't join in the laughter, and he takes the smallest piece of fish, so Elowen frowns and makes him have an extra potato and tells him to stop being such a martyr about everything.

There isn't much, for a family of seven. But what there is tastes like magic to me, fresh and wild and dark as the berries on the vines outside our house. After a while, even Yanny relaxes, and it's kind of wonderful. I'm in a fairy house, deep in Winterspell, having the first big family meal I've ever had. The thought makes me smile, until I notice the shadows at the windows. More, and more of them, leering in, their blank eyes wide, claws scratching at the glass. Elowen notices as I do, and she lowers the lights and draws blinds at the window with a flick of her fingers.

'Stella?'

'The shadows . . .'

Fen's face tightens, and the children are sent to play in their bedroom.

'We don't talk about them,' Yanny says.

'I'm sorry.'

Fen frowns. 'They don't normally cluster like that around the house.' He looks at me, and then to Yanny. 'It's difficult to keep up the barriers, and it was a hard night of fighting last night. I'm sorry.'

'You should let me help,' Yanny says. 'I could do a shift for you sometimes.'

'You are worn thin enough, glamouring all day,' Elowen says, and her tone is sharp. 'They will do us no harm; the house is sound. If they are outside the windows, well, they may wail all they like – they still will not get inside.'

'I don't *have* to go to school.'

'Yes, you do,' Fen says. 'You all do. Whether it is easy or not, you will all do it, and you will get out of here.'

'I don't want to get out of here,' Yanny says quietly. 'This is my home.'

'And I hope it always will be,' says Fen. 'But it has been a decade already, of fighting and hiding, and hoping for change. The Shadow King's subjects are wilder and stronger than ever, so we must make our own changes, prepare for our future. For *your* future.'

'My future is here!'

'Enough of this,' Elowen says. 'Stella doesn't need to hear all of our family dramas. I'll make us a hot drink, and then, Yanny, you can walk Stella home.' A flicker of doubt crosses her face. 'The nights are so dark now, you'll need your faelight.' She looks from Yanny to me and frowns. 'Stella – are you all right?'

'Oh! Yes, of course – I'm sorry. I didn't mean to cause such trouble.'

'You haven't,' she says, her brown eyes glowing with golden flecks. 'You are most welcome here.'

But she doesn't know who I am.

How would she look at me if she did?

The walk through the forest is quiet. Yanny holds the wand-like faelight high above our heads, and mist drizzles through its light, so that a nimbus cloud surrounds us. My fingers find the silver acorn around my neck, and there's reassurance in its familiar weight, even if nothing else is familiar. Even if the shadows crow and call and slither on either side of us.

'Thank you for having me,' I whisper, to distract myself from thin, leering faces and the tread of the shadow wolves by my side.

'It didn't go quite the way I thought.' Yanny sighs, looking sideways at me. 'Nothing ever seems to, around you.'

'I'm sorry things are so difficult here . . .'

'It's fine,' he says. 'What's it like living with ghost nan and a cat and an imp?'

'Ha.' I think about it for a moment, fresh from all the joy and the worry of his home. 'It's quiet. In a good way.'

The roots beneath my feet lurch suddenly, and I'm sent sprawling into the trunk of a slender, still young oak tree, my shoulder jarring hard against it. My breath plumes out in a cloud of steam, and ice crystals fall all around me. A tiny golden shape rolls towards me from the upper reaches of the bank, and I stretch out over the cold earth to grab it as the tree whispers to me of days in the sun.

It's an acorn.

My heart thumps as a flicker of a memory washes over me: my mother, wearing something like this around her neck, its chain catching in her pale hair, smiling as we crouch to pick wild strawberries together . . .

The image is so vivid, it takes me a while to find my feet. I feel like I'm back in that moment, back with her. Yanny stoops to help me up.

'What happened?' he asks, as I brush myself down and pocket the acorn. My hands are trembling, my mind still clinging to that golden summer day. 'You're a liability in here . . .'

'I tripped,' I manage, wrenching myself back to the present. 'Sorry.'

'You can stop saying you're sorry,' he says, his tone strangely gentle. 'None of this is your fault.'

I stare at him. Does he know why I feel so sorry? Have they already guessed that I'm the child of that long-gone fae queen and her tormented husband? That I am this ridiculous Lost Prince who is supposed to know what the heck they're doing and somehow find the cursed palace and stop these nightmare shadows?

'Well, I'm sorry anyway,' I say, and he nods, holding the faelight higher as the shadows creep in closer. They reach for me, and I can feel myself unravelling in here. I clutch the acorn in my pocket.

'What happens if the shadows get you?' I ask.

Yanny flinches but keeps walking. 'If you let them too close, they mess with your head – take you back to things you'd rather forget. If the Stag is around, they're stronger. Then their claws can scratch; their teeth can bite. And they're killing the trees, all the time, more and more.'

'*Killing* them?'

'Lack of light, not good for anything,' he says, but he clearly doesn't want to talk about it any more, and the silence between us is awkward after that, so it's a huge relief when we finally reach the edge of the forest, and I can see my house in the distance. Peg has lit all the lamps, and there's a flicker of silver where the barrier cuts through the night.

'They're waiting for you,' he says with a smile.

'Did you never see our house before today?'

'No,' he says, staring at it now. 'I probably never would have, if you hadn't shown me earlier. Even now, it's a little bit warped-looking. She's a powerful woman, your nan.'

'Will you be OK getting back?' I ask, looking back into the darkness of the forest with a shiver.

'Easier without you, probably,' he says with a grin, turning to head back into the forest.

'See you tomorrow!' I call after him, watching him go, until he's just a thin light in the distance, and Winterspell is thick with writhing, howling shadows. They are men, and bristling wolves, birds, and bats, and tiny insects that cling to the trees. They are wild horses with manes flying, and now a towering stag behind them, his vast antlers proud. He pulls the night sky into his form, and there are stars there too, winking beautiful.

'*Bright thing*,' I hear him whisper, still clear in the distance, and the smiles of all the shadows are moon soft as he steps towards me. My blood rushes cold through my veins as he calls to me, and there's a tiny corner of my mind shouting at me, but he is louder. He is intoxicating. '*Come closer . . .*'

I tread towards him, fighting through young ash, and he rears up with a great bellow, his antlers clashing with the outstretched branches of the trees. And then there are claws on my legs and my back. I scream, and Teacake lands on my shoulder, her fur standing up on end, her tail wrapping around my neck with a bristle of static.

'Ouch! Teacake!'

Her green eyes flare. I stare at her, and then into the forest. The shadows' smiles are not soft now. They are full of teeth. I back away, and they roar, and my knees buckle beneath the tide of their rage, but Teacake swats at me and yowls in my ear, and so I know – I know to turn away. To keep walking, against the pull of their desire, through the mist-thick grass and back to the house. Home to Peg, and to Nan, shivering and half out of my mind with the horror and the pull of those shadows.

There will be hell to pay, but at least it will be the kind of hell that loves me.

16

Nan is waiting by a smouldering fire. For a moment, it's hard to see her, and then she blooms into full view, curled into her armchair. Her arms are folded, and her eyes are narrowed.

'Estelle Brigg,' she says.

'Hey, Nan,' I chirp.

Peg, in his usual spot on the mantelpiece, shakes his head wearily.

I smile sweetly. 'How're you doing?'

'Don't *Hey, Nan* me!' she says, floating a little up into the air. 'Worried, Estelle – *that's* how your old nan is. Peg had the sense to tell me where you'd gone and with whom –' Peg gives me an evil grin – 'so I knew you weren't alone and lost in there. But, Estelle, this is not good enough. You were forbidden from going to school, but there you are. And you were *forbidden* from the forest, for very good reason, and off you pop on a jolly with your friend!'

'It wasn't a jolly!' I snap, my skin still flaring from the close encounter with the shadows, my mind flitting back to Yanny and his weary parents. 'It was a visit with a friend, and you can't expect me to avoid the forest forever.'

'I absolutely *do* expect you to avoid the forest,' she says, her hair puffing out in bright white streaks. 'You know what happened the last time we were in there, Stella – we were lucky to get out alive!'

'But we *did* get out! Other people live in there. They have torches to get through the shadows, they fight them, and we just sit here, hiding in our safe place doing nothing!'

'*Torches* through the shadows?' she says. 'I suppose you mean faelight. How close to the shadows did you get, Estelle?'

I do wish she'd stop calling me Estelle. Once is quite enough of a telling-off.

'Well, they're everywhere, so they got pretty close,' I say, folding my arms. 'Why don't we have a faelight? Why haven't we tried harder?'

'We do have a faelight,' she says, glimmering at the edges with a faint, silvery light of her own. 'We have an old lantern. And we have me – and we have you.

144

The moon sprite in us means we have our own light, Stella. But it still isn't enough! The lantern cracked; the shadows nearly took you whole!'

'But would they have?' I demand. 'Would my father really let the shadows kill me?'

'*Your father!* It is his fault all this is happening! He is blind to it, Stella, hidden away in that palace. He sends his shadow out in search of you, but he sees nothing. Nothing but his own despair.'

'His *shadow*?'

'He could always do it.' She sighs. 'And I named him Ellos, which means *stag*, so that is the shape his shadow takes.'

I sit down with a thump on to the bench, my stomach hollow.

'Stella?'

'I saw it.'

'You saw the Stag?'

The room is utterly quiet, save for the ticking of the clock. The air grows thick with it.

'How close did he get? Did he speak to you, Stella?'

'He . . . might have said something about a bright thing,' I say.

She rises from her chair in outrage. 'Oh, STELLA!

What have you done?' She puts her hands up to her mouth, staring at me.

'You never told me his shadow was out there! That it was looking for me!'

'I was trying to protect you – I promised your mother I'd keep you safe, and that stag, that *creature* who was your father, he is long gone, Stella. He died the day your mother died; he caught the Plaga himself, and it weakened him, and then the grief . . . he is not my Ellos. He is not a creature who can care for you, and so I kept you away, as much as I could, to keep you safe. You're not thirteen yet, you are not in your full power, Estelle. You're still a child!'

My mind is a fog of too many things whirring. I sit on the bench and wrap my fingers around the warm, solid edge of it.

'How is it safe to keep secrets? Why were you trying to keep me imprisoned here? Did you really think I wouldn't ever find the company of humans, or fae? Did you want me to be alone here forever?'

'You are not alone!'

She's shouting now, and it's the first time I've ever heard her do it. Peg covers his ears, as the fire starts popping, and Teacake curls up into a ball on the rug.

'*I* am here. And Peg. And this little cat of yours!'

'But no *friends*, Nan. No people!'

'Mrs Mandrake is people,' she mutters, but the heat has gone, as quick as it came, and now she just looks tired, and I feel bad.

'Speaking of secrets,' she says after a moment. 'Peg tells me this Yanny is one of your school friends.'

'Ah . . . yes. He is.'

'Then there is magic at the school?'

I wince. 'Some of the kids are from Winterspell. I didn't know that when I started.'

'But you found out. And you lied to me.'

'I just didn't tell you. I didn't want to worry you.'

'Didn't want to worry me!' She snorts. 'You've worried me since the day I brought you here. All of my care, and you just waltz in and put yourself right in the middle of it all. This is why I warned you against going, Stella – it's too soon. I *knew* it would be trouble.'

'Well I've done it now, and there's no going back,' I say, my fingers finding the golden acorn in my pocket. 'I'm glad I'm at school, and I'm glad I've been into Winterspell.' I take a deep breath. 'I think I miss them, Nan.'

'Who?'

'My parents! Being in Winterspell. I remember things in flashes . . . I wish I knew more.'

'Of course you do,' she says, her eyes glowing. 'I wish it too. I've wished it many times over the years.'

'But we don't talk about them much.'

'I suppose we don't,' she acknowledges, twisting her hands together. 'Well, then. Your mother was a moon sprite, like my own mother. She made the most beautiful dreams – and most of the charms that I brought with me and strung out there on the fence. And your father is known, apart from anything else, as the wood sprite fae king who made the bridge that crosses the River Bat, deep in the forest; who linked up all the charms and invented warning systems, that I have used to keep us safe from him. They were happy, before the Plaga struck. You were happy.'

Fingering the acorn in my pocket, I think of the whisper of the oak tree, that memory of summer days, and how its roots threw me over. 'Is his tree still alive?'

'It's in the forest,' she says. 'It's an oak, still young.' She sighs, and her sadness looms over us both.

'I think I saw it,' I say.

'Perhaps you did.' She shakes her head. 'They can survive without us far better than we can live without them. But for now, have you not had enough adventure?'

'No! I've hardly begun, Nan! *We* should live in the forest. We should drop all this glamour and go in there and fight with the rest of them. I want to know who I *am*! I don't even look fae . . . What about wings – and horns?'

'Wings and horns!' she exclaims. 'As to that, you can thank me. You don't have to use your own glamour to go into the town, or to school, because I did it for you years ago.'

'But what am I, underneath all of your glamour? What do I have that you have hidden?'

'I forget.'

'NAN! How can you *forget*?'

'All of my energy is spent on the here and now, Stella! You will come into your magic, and when you do, the glamour will fall. That is always how I intended it. I . . .' For a second, she looks utterly lost. 'There are many choices in raising a child. I can't say I've always made the right one.'

'It's terrible in the forest,' I say after a while, when the fire is low, and Peg is 'awake' again. I've decided to tell them both a bit about Yanny and his family, and as I do, I feel again the gnawing worry that showed in his parents' eyes.

'And their wings – his parents' wings – are faded and all folded away. And the kids' wings are like shadows – like they're not really there at all.'

Nan considers, her face drawn with tiredness. If I demand too much of her, will she leave? I know she wouldn't mean to, but if she gets too thin, would she just disappear?

'I suppose it may be part of the shadow curse. Since the shadows took over, there is little light, little to eat. They have always concealed them, of course, when they're glamouring, but in their own world . . . I don't know, Stella. I can't fix it all . . . ' She stares at me. 'And you're still so young. I wanted to protect you from it. Who knows what you've set off now. You should've just stayed away. I was charged with bringing you up safely.' She says it almost to herself. 'I tried to find the palace. For years, I dragged you in there. I thought that if we found him, we could wake him to reality, but I saw how much it took from you – how strong the shadows were around you. Your presence made it worse. We had to stay away. And now you go walking right into their lair!'

'Maybe . . . it's time,' I say, keeping my voice low.

She winces. 'You're still a child.'

'What does that mean? That I'm powerless? You know that's not true, Nan.'

'But you don't know enough. You aren't strong enough.'

'So I'll keep going to school – to learn. And to have friends.'

'You'll stay away from the forest? Please, Stella – promise me you'll stay away. You may be right; the time may be drawing closer. But looking at you now, I don't think it's here yet.' She fixes her gaze on me. 'I don't think you're ready to face your father. Memories are wonderful things, they are precious, but he is not the same fae king that you have in your mind. He changed, Stella, more completely than I have ever seen any creature change. You must be ware of him, and of that stag shadow of his. Will you hear me, Stella? Will you be ware? Have your school, have your friends, but don't let them know you're the child of the Shadow King – and stay away from that forest!'

I look down at myself. Covered in mud and bits of bramble, my hands shaking, my stomach a horrible, empty dark place where fears have gathered deep as shadows. I don't know how to fight them, yet. I don't even know how to keep from falling on my face in there.

'Do you think they'd hate me if they knew who I was?'

'They wouldn't hate you,' Nan says, drawing closer. 'They don't know you, Stella. They don't know my lovely girl, for all that she is. But they might be unwelcoming. Until you are strong in your power, all you'll be is a reminder of him.'

'I'll stay away for now,' I whisper, closing my eyes and seeing flashes of monstrous teeth and claws.

When I open my eyes, she's gone. I stand up and dig my hands into my pocket and draw out the golden acorn. It's almost identical to my own silver one. I bring the chain out from under my shirt and hold them side by side. There's a twist in the air, and they snap together. The gold one disappears, and when I hold the silver one up to the light, I can see new gold strands, a fine lace of them at the top of the acorn.

'Well look at that!' Peg whistles. 'Your mother's acorn – how did you find it?'

'I think it found me,' I say in a whisper. 'I got tripped up by a tree – my father's oak – and . . . there it was on the ground. I didn't know it was out there to find.

Did you know it was out there, Peg? Why didn't you say anything? What does it mean?'

'Couldn't. Not my place. And what would you have done, anyway? It came to you when the time was right, as these things do. You're only just big enough to discover these things now.'

'I've been bigger than you for years!'

'That's on the outside,' he sniffs. 'I'm talking about the inside.'

The Troll

Glitter-skinned and solid as the oak in form and quiet determination, the troll is a peaceful creature, known for its wisdom more than for its fight. It has strong, powerful wings, but it rarely uses them, for the motion causes great upheaval. In dire circumstances, however, there is no better creature to have on your side. The troll is a cunning strategist and not afraid to use all that he has, if only the cause is great enough.

FIGHT – 6

FLIGHT – 7

MAGIC – 5

DISGUISE – 9

17

Mr Flint, with his sweeping, glittering wings, is in a temper, his eyes glowing like coals. In fae ethics, everyone gets very intense about fae politics and the situation in the forest, and I try to keep my head down, but today's lesson seems to be mostly about instilling fear, and Mr Flint is very good at that.

'You are here to learn how to assimilate yourselves, not because it's a party out there in the human world . . .' He catches a couple of the kids chatting and raises his voice. 'But because your own world is a *battleground*. So you will learn to assimilate. You will learn to hide your magic with your glamour. And you will go out there, and you will make a difference!'

'And leave our families in Winterspell?' Tash demands. 'And do what? I don't want to assimilate. There is nothing I need from the human world!' She flashes her silver teeth.

'Silly girl,' he growls. 'You need to survive. You need to learn how their world works so that you can help your family, and everybody who will remain in the forest. You have a choice! Not all do. The centaurs, the goblins, many of my troll brethren – they do not have the ability to glamour. They need the forest to remain. You must help to influence others in that vein.'

'The forest isn't under threat from humanity,' Yanny says quietly. 'It's under threat from the shadows.'

'And we will win that battle,' Mr Flint says, slamming a hand down on the desk. It cracks and then folds like a pack of cards beneath his touch. His eyes glow. 'There is no greater priority among the fae council. What you must do is survive it so that we all may survive the bigger fight: to keep the forest whole.'

Nobody answers this time, and Mr Flint's anger has been burned out. He sighs down at the pile of rubble that was a desk a moment ago, and herds everybody into the adjoining room: a huge redbrick space with a high ceiling and polished wood floor, where the self-defence and spell-craft lessons are held. He's filling in for the usual teacher today, and as his eyes flash around the room, I can tell he's not going to make it easy for anybody.

'So,' he says, lifting himself to the wooden platform in the centre with a leathery flap of his wings. 'Let's see what you have been learning with Ms Elder. Tash and Stella – come on.'

My skin flares as Tash turns her silver eyes on me, mounting the platform with a nimble leap. I follow, using my hands to pull myself up and clambering on, knee-first. By the time I've picked myself up, she's standing, feet planted wide, and of course everybody is staring at us. She pulls the ice-blue needles from her hair, never taking her eyes off me, and begins to advance.

Last time, I just stood at the back of the class and watched.

I glance over at Mr Flint, wondering what he thinks I'm going to do, but he just returns my gaze and folds his arms, so I guess it's up to me. Thing is, I don't have flashing blue hair needles, or fiery eyes – I don't have anything. I spent most of last night either pacing my room, full of rage at Nan and Peg and the world in general for making things so complicated, or looking at myself, trying to uncover my fae-ness. I said all the familiar spell words with a new zing, wondering if my magic would suddenly burst forth, especially now that my mother's acorn has merged with my own, but they didn't act any differently. I don't even have interesting teeth.

Tash grins. 'Ready?'

'Yes,' I snap, gathering myself and muttering Nan's words for self-defence. She was always very bossy about self-defence. I just wish she'd taught me a few words of attack as well.

Tash dances forward, clearly determined to find a chink in my armour, but she's too angry to do it with any subtlety; her eyes flash like mirrors before she strikes with the lightning magic in her needles, and her next move is pretty easy to read. I keep on murmuring the words under my breath, and my clumsy feet don't let me fall. At one point, there's even a flash of something that didn't come from Tash – it's there and gone again so quickly that I'm not entirely sure what happened, but Tash's eyes widen in surprise, and after that she's more cautious.

'Very good!' Mr Flint calls out, halting us before I can work out what I did or whether I can do it again.

The acorn at my throat is uncomfortably warm, and I'm fairly sure it did *something* in there.

'Let's change. Excellent defence work, Stella – not at all bad for your first time. Let's have you out. Tash, you're getting pretty nifty with those needles – though you need to remember not to rely upon them alone. It is *your power* that drives *them*, not the other way around!'

He calls Yanny up to face Tash next, and he's pretty excellent at the fight. His smoke lingers in the air, and he has a fiery whip that curls around his wrist and snaps in the air. Mr Flint pits student after student against him, but nobody stands for long, until another girl – Laurel – steps in, and they parry with hot words and quick, dancing feet, his whip against the nimble flick of her slim wooden staff, until finally Yanny holds up his hands in defeat – through tiredness if nothing else, by the look of him.

'You spread yourself too thin, boy!' Mr Flint snaps from the sidelines. 'You need to control it better; rage will only carry you so far!'

Yanny nods, tight-lipped, as we're dismissed.

'Are you OK?' I ask him once the lesson is over, while he fixes his glamour out in the corridor. I can feel the stretch of magic in the air, it's thin, dangerous.

'Yep,' he says, rolling his shoulders as we step through the wooden door and head down the stairs.

'That was intense.'

He shrugs. 'Yep.'

I don't know what to say, how to make him feel better. He looks utterly worn out, and there's a tension around him that makes me anxious. I guess there's probably nothing I can do right now.

I keep close though, all morning, and Zara senses something too. She doesn't comment, but I know she's worried. We get through double English, and then it's maths, and the winter sun streams through the windows, making patches of searing light across the desks. The radiators are on full blast, and Yanny is struggling, his skin pale beneath bright freckles. I whisper the words of heart, to lend him strength – and for a while, it seems to work. He picks up his pen, fixes his attention on the page before him. But as soon as I'm done with the spell, his hand stills, and he wilts back into the chair.

'Yanny –' Zara leans into him – 'concentrate.'

He sits upright and pulls the book closer.

'Here,' she says, shaking her head as she flips the pages. 'That one. Look, I'll help you with it later. Just look busy for a minute – Mr Goodenough is on the warpath.'

And he is, his blue eyes flashing around the classroom

as if looking for a target. Yanny bends low over his book, as if deep in study, but his eyes are unfocused. Zara frowns over at me.

'Just say he's ill or something,' I whisper.

'Mr G doesn't care about that!'

'Well, he should.'

'Yanny's already on a warning. He fell asleep in his lesson last week. Most of the teachers don't seem to mind, but Mr G does.'

'He'll be OK,' I whisper. 'There's only ten minutes left . . .'

I reach deep for new words, thinking of the spell Nan taught me for fortitude. I look down at my own book and mutter the words slowly. They unwind from me, and I can feel the power in them. Yanny stirs next to me, and I keep muttering, until the bell goes, ignoring increasingly quizzical looks from Zara.

'OK! The next chapter for homework, please,' says Mr Goodenough. 'Off you go, slowly. Remember your coats – and I expect better next time!'

He pins me with a stare, and I nod, turning to pack my things, feeling a bit fuzzy-headed.

We scuttle out of the room and head to the cafeteria, but I can't keep the words going in the rabble of the corridor, and Yanny starts weaving erratically, his eyes flashing.

'What is your deal?' Zara demands. 'Yanny? Stella? What's going on?'

'I'll take him to the, uh, medical room,' I say.

'The medical room?'

'Upstairs.'

She looks between us warily. 'I'll help.'

'No. Leave it with me.'

'Stella, no. Please don't do this – don't exclude me. I know there's something going on—'

Yanny collides with a glass door and starts to giggle. Out of the corner of my eye, I see Tash charging up the steps, a determined look on her face. If she reports that he's out of control down here . . .

'Zara, I'll explain later, but we have to go. I'm sorry.'

'Go on, then!' she bursts, steadying Yanny as he stumbles into us. 'Go! I'll wait right here.'

She sits on the bottom of the steps as I hustle Yanny up them and through the charms and the double doors. He's hot as a small sun, and his shadow boils across the wall as we go. When we reach the time-out room, he staggers and pretty much falls into one of the chairs, and the change is instant.

He is no human.

Fae, through and through, pupils wide and flecked with fire, the outline of his would-be wings clear against the fabric of the chair behind him. His breath steams out as he lets go of the glamour, and his eyes drift closed. I fetch water and perch on the chair next to his, and then Tash strides in with Principal Ashworth.

'Look!' she exclaims. 'Look at the state of him. Wild, he was, downstairs.'

'He's fine,' I say. 'He's just tired.'

'Well he's here now, and I've heard no alarm. We'll entrust Stella with his care, shall we, Tash?' Principal Ashworth says, casting a dark look at her.

'It's not safe, him being like that around people. He could expose us all.'

'If you are exposed, young lady, it will be your own doing. Now, I have business to see to, and I suggest that you go and find some lunch.' Principal Ashworth stares at her until she backs down and flounces out of the room.

He turns his attention to me. 'Well done for getting him up here. Yanny is rather overtaxed at the moment.' He looks down at him with a frown. 'I'm glad he has a friend, Stella. Let me know if there's anything I can do.'

I nod, and he bustles out again.

I take a deep, steadying breath, thankful there's nobody else in the room. I don't know what to do next, and Yanny certainly isn't going to pass for human any time soon, but at least it's quiet in here.

Until Zara bounces in.

'This place is awesome. I snuck in as Tash was leaving. She didn't even see me, she was in such a strop. What's going on, Stella? What do you all do up here?'

'Oh, Zara! You're not allowed up here – there's going to be trouble!'

She scowls at me. 'Well. There's already trouble, I'd say, and you'd think it would be good to have a friend here to help you. I don't care what's happening, so long as you let me help. What *is* going on with Yanny? I've seen him tired before, and he gets clumsy, but that was something else entirely!'

She looks down at him, and her eyes widen.

'Stella! What . . .'

'He's a fairy,' I say.

'But –' She sits hard on the chair next to him. 'But –' She stares around the room, her eyes widening at the ethereal glow of the lights in the walls, the silver charms set up high. 'Oh. But I . . . But –' She stares at Yanny. 'What happened to his wings?'

'It's part of the shadow curse, I think . . . I don't know. I'll explain what I can later, we just need to get him through the afternoon, and then get him home.'

'How can he go to lessons like this?'

'I can't,' Yanny says with a grin, steam escaping from between his teeth.

Zara flinches, but she sits firm.

'What happened?' I ask. 'Why are you so . . . fae?'

'The glamouring's a bit shaky,' he says, his eyes still closed. 'I was on watch last night. I thought I could manage. Then Laurel got to me when we were duelling.'

'Did she hurt you?'

'No! I'm just tired.'

'I didn't think you were allowed to go on watch,' I say.

'*Watch?*' Zara mouths, but I shake my head.

'Later, Zara!'

'Did it anyway,' he murmurs. 'And it was fine, the fight was good, but today the . . . the stitches kept coming undone. I couldn't keep the ends together . . .'

I shake my head. 'What do you need?'

'Mrs Mandrake.'

'Mrs Mandrake? *My* Mrs Mandrake?'

'I don't know whose she is,' he says, blinking. His

pupils have filled his eyes, and Zara swallows hard as she sees it. 'Pa said . . . I should call her, in an emergency.' He grabs for his bag, but it falls to the floor, and steam billows from his mouth as he hisses with frustration.

'Let me,' Zara says, pushing him back. She reaches down and starts rummaging in the pockets of the bag, eventually finding a crumpled piece of paper with a number on it. She gets out her phone and dials with no hesitation and speaks quick and firm.

'She's on her way,' she says.

'Oh good,' says Yanny. 'That'll be trouble later.'

'Never mind later. We need to fix you now,' she says.

'OK,' he whispers, closing his eyes.

Zara gives a low whistle, staring from him to me. 'I mean, I knew there was stuff going on, and I *knew* magic was real, but what is all this? It's a nightmare! How are you involved, Stella? What's going on?'

'Let's just . . . get through this, and I'll tell you – I promise.' I hold her gaze and take a deep breath, seeing Nan and Peg in my mind, how horrified they're going to be, and saying it anyway: 'You can come to mine after school.'

She nods. 'OK.'

*

Mrs Mandrake raises an eyebrow in surprise when she sees us all sitting there. I smile, but it feels a bit hopeless.

'Stella. Glad to see you're making friends,' she says. 'This must be the Zara your nan spoke about. What a fine mess you've got yourself caught up in, my girl. And here is Yanny.' She frowns, taking in his form. 'It's a good job you called.' She starts rummaging in her bag, eventually coming out with a small purse.

I open my mouth to say something. Anything. But nothing comes out.

'We'll talk later,' she says. 'Let's get this boy sorted out for now.' She stares at him for a moment, noting aloud the steam coming from his nostrils, the monochrome of his complexion.

She looks up at me. 'His eyes – how do they look?'

'Um. Fiery. Then his pupils sort of filled them.'

She tuts and unzips a small purse, using tiny silver tweezers to draw out a bunch of very smelly dried twigs.

'What's that? Is he going to be OK?' asks Zara.

'Oh yes –' she shakes her head – 'for now, anyway.'

She looks angry in a way I've never seen before. She takes a deep breath and thrusts the bundle under Yanny's nose. His eyes snap open, and he tries to jerk away, but she holds him firm, her mouth a set line, and slowly whatever she's doing begins to work. He is still very clearly unhuman, but colour starts to bleed back into his skin.

'OK,' she says. 'That'll do it.'

'What was that twig thing?'

'Bit of a mer-fae nest,' she says. 'He's been overdoing it. Keeping up the glamour is a tall order when you're half-starved and sleep deprived, never mind all that fighting he's been doing in there. I've just calmed it all down a bit and restored a little of his energy. Now – I've got to go. I'll go and see Principal Ashworth now and make sure you're not disturbed. I'll tell him that I've allowed you in here, Zara – that should save you all some trouble. We should talk, you and I . . .' She looks at Zara long and hard, as if making her mind up about something. 'Yes, we should. Now, get Yanny home once the coast is clear, and make sure he rests. *No* glamouring for him, not for a good few days.'

And with that, she's gone, leaving us with a very confused, bleary-eyed Yanny.

'Well, *she's* pretty awesome,' Zara says. 'Is she human?'

'Yes.'

'So humans can have magic of their own . . .'

'Course they can,' whispers Yanny. 'If they want to.'

He chuckles to himself, steam still billowing.

'Is this what he usually looks like?' Zara whispers.

'Yes, when he's not using a glamour to disguise himself.'

'What about you?' she asks, staring me up and down. 'Are you like Mrs Mandrake?'

Yanny laughs harder, and the wisps of his wings glow orange. I glower at him.

'No,' I say. 'I'm . . . a bit more like Yanny.'

'But it doesn't show?'

'It's a long story.' I try a smile at her, though it feels wobbly – everything feels very precarious right now. Will she mind that I haven't already told her? 'Can we talk about it later, once we're out of here?'

'Yes,' she says. 'And you don't need to look so panicked about it. I *knew* there was something different about both of you. Now, how are we going to get him out of here without anyone noticing?'

'We wait until the last bell goes. And then we'll just have to go for it.'

'Stella can glamour for me,' Yanny says, stumbling to his feet. 'Come on. I need to get out of here now.' He looks at Zara. 'You found your way up, then.' He gives a broad smile. 'Knew you would, one day.'

'You could've told me,' she says.

'No.' He shakes his head sadly. 'Not allowed. Nor was Stella.'

'It was Tash who let her in,' I say. 'But that's beside the point. Principal Ashworth said there were life-and-death exceptions – and you did look pretty deathly – and Mrs Mandrake said she'd sort it. For now, we need to work out what we're going to do with you – I can't glamour!'

'Oh you can,' he says tiredly. 'Just try, please? I need to get home.'

'I've never done it before though – I've never needed to!'

'Lucky you,' he says. He picks up his bag with a grunt and stands in front of us, pale and swaying on his feet, his expression utterly determined. 'Come on. Let's go.'

He tears through the corridor, bangs out through the double doors, and careers down the stairs. Fortunately most of the kids are in lessons, only a couple rushing late, so we charge out with him, through reception, past a startled Mrs Edge, and into the clear, cool air of the mid-afternoon. Yanny sags a little as we reach the school gate, but his pace doesn't falter, and so we head off towards town.

'Just cover me,' he says as we start off down the street. His would-be wings are like dark smoke, the whole sense of him is fierce, fragile, and unmistakeably one hundred per cent fae.

'I don't know how to glamour!' I howl.

'Wait a minute,' says Zara, stopping him with her hand. 'Yanny. Stop.'

'Zara—'

'Don't Zara me. You kept huge secrets, even though I told you all my stuff. I trusted you, Yanny. You were the only person I told about my . . . the separation, when I moved here. And you hid all *this*! So I am being understanding, I am being a virtual SAINT about it all, but that's enough. You can't just command someone else to do something they're uncomfortable with and expect me to go along with it.'

'She can do it!'

'That isn't the point!'

'What – she won't? Fine, then. I'll just go on my own. Hardly anyone about anyway. Who cares?'

'I care,' I say. 'And I'll do it, if I can, but I never have before, and I don't know how, so you'll have to teach me!'

'Your words. Your spells. You've used them before, in

class . . . You use them more than you think. And you tell yourself they're just words, but they're not. They're the language of magic, and they're powered by the magic in you. *That's* what you need to use.'

'I don't know the words for glamouring . . .'

'There aren't any,' he says. 'You just need to feel it. Imagine a barrier between us and the world, see the picture you want everybody else to see, and live in it.'

Zara frowns. 'What? How's she supposed to *live in it*?'

But I get it. I know the feeling he's talking about. I know about barriers. All the things in our own barrier around our house, they're just moments of thought, symbols of power. Perhaps I can make my own, without the silver.

'You'll have to judge it,' I say to Zara. 'Stand clear . . . and let me know if anything changes.'

I stare at Yanny and see him as he is, but also as he makes himself. A little shorter; a little more stout. No wings. Skin and hair, warmer; eyes, less bright; teeth, less sharp. It occurs to me as I'm doing it that I'm diluting the best bits of him, but I push the thought away. It's distracting.

172

'Well?' I ask Zara, my mind fragmented.

She stares at us.

'Zara!'

The work I've done on Yanny evaporates.

'Yes!' she says. 'Sorry. I was pinching myself. You did it. I mean it was a bit wobbly, and you made him a bit short, but to a casual passer-by . . .' She shrugs. 'He'd pass.'

I pull all my thoughts together again, and something Yanny said earlier, about the stitches coming undone, suddenly makes sense. It is like stitching something; a new reality. One piece of deception leads to another, and if you lose yourself halfway, the whole thing sort of collapses. Yanny is uncharacteristically patient while I work; he looks utterly spent.

'There,' I whisper. 'Got it?'

'You've got it,' Zara says, leaning in and taking hold of Yanny's hand. 'Come on. March.'

We wrangle ourselves through the town centre, huddling up tight to each other, avoiding the gaze of anyone we meet. A couple of dogs definitely notice there's something unusual going on and give us a wide berth, but the people we pass don't seem to see anything out of place.

We trail around the edge of town, and make our way out on the river path, towards my house and the forest, but as we go, it starts to get harder to see the glamour on him, and he is mostly sleepwalking, leaning into Zara while I focus my energy on seeing him the right way.

'OK?' Zara asks after a while, as we head further out of town.

'Mm,' I manage. 'Nearly there . . .' But as I say it, I realize I can't get us into the forest past the shadows with him like this, even if his faelight works. My mind is buzzing with the effort of hiding him already. We can't leave him there to find his way through by himself. There's only one place we can safely go now.

Home.

I look at Zara. It's probably time for an explanation.

The Mer-Fae

Moon-worshippers, water-breathers. Silver-skinned, and teeth sharp as the finest tailor's needle. The mer-fae are fierce, and wild, and better avoided. Legend of them is thin, tattered like old lace, for they keep to the deep, dark waters of the lakes that lap at the ancient yew, and they rise only in a blood moon.

Their song is sorrowful, for they do not recognize the passing of time, and every time they walk the solid earth that man has claimed, it is diminished. Flee, man-child, from the mer-fae. Its mirror eyes will make all the world a shimmering dream from which you'll never wake.

FIGHT – 10

FLIGHT – 0

MAGIC – 9

DISGUISE – 0

18

'We'll go to mine,' I say, as we get to the top of the hill, and the house comes into view down below, just before the forest and the slow swell of the mountain. 'Nan will know what to do.'

'Ghost Nan?' asks Yanny.

'Stella?' Zara stares at us both. 'What now?'

I take a deep breath. 'The forest isn't haunted; it's full of shadows because the old fae king is mad with grief. He locked himself away in his palace and cursed it so that nobody could get close – nobody could even find it – and the shadows he made with all his sorrow invaded Winterspell. So all the fae are fighting with the shadows and living underground, and the trees are dying as the shadows spread. It's all part of the Shadow King's curse. My nan says that's maybe why Yanny's wings are the way they are – the shadows blight everything.'

'*And . . .*' She looks between us wildly, tucking her

hair behind her ears, clearing her throat. 'Let's say I've got all that. For now. What was Yanny saying about *ghost Nan*?'

'Ah yes. And my nan is a ghost who is getting thinner by the day.'

Yanny laughs, and Zara stares, and I can just *feel* the swift tick of her mind, working it all out, recognizing the truth of it. She sits down on the side of the hill, pulling me and Yanny with her on to the cold, scrubby ground.

'Is it just you and her?'

'And Peg. He's, um . . .'

'Um what?' she persists.

My mind whirrs, but it's never going to win against Zara. I look at Yanny, but he's leaning back on his elbows, eyes closed, face tipped to the darkening sky.

'He's an imp.'

She slaps me on the arm, and then claps her hands. 'IMPS ARE REAL!'

'Don't *shout* about it!'

'No. OK.' She bounces a bit, clasping her hands together. Then she turns her full bright on me again, and it makes me laugh.

'What about you?'

'What about me?'

'What kind of fairy are you?'

'Not a fairy,' I say. 'I'm a sprite.'

'A sprite,' she breathes, staring at me, her head on one side. 'I thought they were smaller.'

'I don't think they are,' I say, looking down at myself. 'Nan cast a glamour over me when I was small, and I haven't worked out how to break it yet, so I don't really know . . .'

'Not a lot smaller,' says Yanny. 'Pretty much the same as fairies, only not so clever, and not so good in battle.'

'Yanny!'

'S'true,' he says, shaking his head sadly.

'You're delirious. I'll show you, when I can work out how. I'm sure I can fight just as much as you can.'

'So why haven't you?' he asks, his eyes still bleary.

'I wasn't allowed to. Nan says she was protecting me.' I shrug, knowing it's cowardly. Yanny wasn't allowed to either, only he did.

'And your nan,' Zara says, frowning. 'Ghost Nan. She's getting thin?'

'She died a long time ago . . . She came back to look after me when my mother died. She's OK, just . . . Yeah, a bit worn out sometimes.' I shrug, trying to make it sound like it's all OK, and nothing to be so sad about.

But I am so sad about it.

When I see her getting thinner, when I see how exhausted she looks – when she disappears entirely, even if it's just for a couple of hours – it's terrible. I thought she'd be with me forever. It seemed only right, since the rest of my family is such a disaster. She does always come back, I remind myself. And she always says she'll hang around for as long as I need her to. The way things are at the moment, she'll see that being for a *long* time.

'So, ghost Nan looks after you?'

I press my fingers into the earth.

'Yeah. And Peg. And I have a new little cat called Teacake . . .'

Zara's eyes get all soft, and I wish I could take it back, because I just want to see the bright of her excitement, and now it's gone.

'You and Yanny have been hiding whole worlds from me! Whole . . . magical worlds.' She stares out at Cloudfell Mountain and the dark swathe of Winterspell.

I wince. 'I know.'

'And now I'm supposed to be all noble and understanding?' She sighs.

'You *are* noble and understanding,' I say.

'Why didn't you say something when I was asking before?'

'I didn't know what to say. I didn't realize there were fae at school, or magic lessons. I just wanted to be normal.'

'Normal!' She shakes her head. 'Who's normal? What's normal?'

'I don't know! I thought that school would be, I suppose. I'm sorry I didn't say anything. I'm glad you know now. Are you OK? Do you still want to come with us?'

'I do!' she says, reaching in her bag for her phone. 'I'll just have to text Mum to let her know I'll be home late.'

I watch her screen light up with an instant reply that's more kisses than words, and Zara smiles, tucking it back into her bag. She catches me watching.

'OK?' she whispers.

I look towards home, where smoke is curling from the chimney, and people – or at least creatures – are waiting for me.

I smile back. 'Yeah.'

'Cold,' whispers Yanny, sitting up and folding into his knees, shivering as a bitter November rain begins to fall. 'I'm cold. Can we move, please?'

'Come on, then,' I say, steeling myself.

I don't have a phone, and neither does Nan – the very idea is comical – so there's no way to warn her of what's coming her way. We'll just have to deal with it. Zara and I help Yanny to his feet, and we run down the hill, slipping and sliding through the mud, spattering our clothes as the rain gets stronger. By the time we reach the garden, our breathless shouts have turned to laughter, and then we hit the barriers, and of course Yanny's presence sets off all the alarms.

I wonder why mine don't. I suppose it's Nan's super-glamour. Or maybe the spell allows for me, since I live there. I shake my head and unwind the silver wire to let us all through, speaking the words of peace, and then we rush for the door, bursting into the bright kitchen before I'm really ready.

Nan, Peg and Teacake are all in there, sitting around the fireplace. Teacake has a saucer of milk on the rug; Peg is being a bird, sitting innocently by a mug of hot chocolate. They look up as Zara and I collide on the doormat, suddenly aware of muddy shoes and dripping coats. Yanny staggers through, careless, dropping on to the bench and holding his hands out to the fire.

'Stella?' Nan demands, rising from her armchair.

'This is Zara, and that's Yanny. He's a fairy, I told you about him. He's a bit . . . under the weather. Zara's a human. They're my new school friends. Um, Zara, this is my nan. And that's Peg up on the mantelpiece . . . And that's Teacake.'

Teacake looks up from her milk. Yanny whistles. Everybody stares at me. I give them a toothy sort of smile, while my stomach churns, and my skin prickles with heat.

'What's wrong with your fairy friend?' Nan asks eventually.

'He was a bit run-down, and his glamouring got out of control. Mrs Mandrake used a bit of mer-fae nest to revive him!'

'She's very good in an emergency,' says Nan. 'Always has been.'

'Did you know she could do that?'

'Of course!' says Nan. 'Most humans have a little fae in them, if they open their minds to it – and the closer to Winterspell you are, the easier that is . . . But now, tell me the rest of the story. You all look highly hassled.'

'We're OK. And Yanny's better than he was, thanks to Mrs Mandrake, but I had to do the glamouring for him through town, and it was all a bit of a struggle, and so . . . I thought we'd stop here before we get him home.'

'Well at least you got that bit right,' says Nan. 'Glamouring, eh? And it worked?'

'Yes.'

'She did a great job,' Zara says brightly.

Nan blinks. 'Well. Good. You all look wrung out from your adventures, I must say. Food is what we need now.'

She gives me a long, stern look so I know we'll be talking again later, but for now, she seems happy enough to boss me and Zara around the kitchen. We make spaghetti with garlic and fresh tomatoes, and green beans from the garden. Zara flits about with me, her eyes filled with wonder at everything; even the battered old colander is charming and needs inspecting. Teacake remains curled before the fire while we cook, and Peg watches it all closely from the mantelpiece, occasionally sending sparks up the chimney with a flutter of his wings. Nan billows around us, and she's just as bossy and chiding with Zara as she is with me, but the more she does it, the brighter Zara glows.

When dinner is ready, we set the table together, and suddenly it hits me that I've never done this before. Never had to lay the table for more than just me. Yanny stirs and stumbles up, fetching salt and pepper, raiding the drawer for the old steel cutlery and sending it flashing across the table.

And then we sit. Yanny, Zara and I, and Peg with his special old tin plate in one corner of the table; Teacake with her gold-rimmed saucer in another.

'You said you have an imp?' whispers Zara.

Peg fixes his dark bird eyes on me.

I shrug. 'He's good at disguise.'

'It's the bird,' Yanny says with a yawn, picking up his cutlery and spearing a strand of spaghetti with the fork. 'Imps like being birds. They like to fly; they like to look down on others.'

'Ridiculous,' says Peg.

Zara stares, her eyes wide as saucers.

'Go on, show her,' says Yanny. 'She's already seen plenty today; it's a bit late to be pretending it all isn't real.'

Peg growls, his form blurring, stretching and re-forming.

'Wow,' says Zara.

'Isn't he lovely,' Nan says with a smile.

'You'd better tell us what you've got planned next,' says Peg around a mouthful of food. Teacake eyes his tail as it swats against the table, and before I can do anything, she's pounced on it.

Peg squeals, jumping up and swiping at her; Nan is so surprised, she loses her grip on her chair and floats up into the air; and I start flapping about, trying to separate the kitten from the imp. Yanny watches this all with a delighted grin on his face, and Zara beams.

'Amazing,' she whispers, amid the smash of plates on the floor, the silver whirl of cutlery as Peg whips his tail across the table. Teacake jumps up and clings to the candelabra, swinging from the ceiling, sending beams of light and shards of shadow across the room. Nan has virtually disappeared in the chaos.

'Enough!' I shout, grabbing Teacake and pulling her on to my lap. The kitchen slowly settles. 'We need to work out how to get Yanny home.'

'I can just walk?' he says, taking another wedge of bread from the dish in the middle of the table. His plate is sparkling clean already, and he does look a lot better.

'Not on your own,' says Zara.

'Who made you the boss?' he demands. 'I'm fine now.

Thank you for your help, but I am perfectly capable of making my way home all by myself.'

'Your judgement is impaired,' I say.

'And Mrs Mandrake said you can't glamour for a few days . . .' adds Zara.

'I don't need to glamour just to get home. It's only over there.' He points vaguely in the direction of the back door.

'But –' Nan sighs, collecting herself and sitting back at the table, her face serious as she stares at me before turning to him – 'you shouldn't go in alone if you are unwell. Stella and Zara can join you.' Her gaze lingers on the curve of his would-be wings. 'I would come if I could, but my time has passed for that. Perhaps Peg could travel with you all.'

'Ah, no,' says Peg. 'I'll keep the boundaries here. The nights are getting longer, and the shadows stretch further these days.'

He never did tell me why he's not allowed in there – I forgot in all the drama of finding my mother's acorn and meeting my father's shadow. But it doesn't seem quite the time to ask right now.

'Is it safe for Zara?' I ask Nan. I can't quite believe she's OK with me going in there. She isn't, I realize, as I look at her. She's pale, and her edges are tattered, almost vibrating. She isn't OK with it at all. It's just that there's no better option. 'I mean, with her being human . . .'

'Safer,' Nan says. 'The shadows won't have any hold over her. In fact, she's about the best company you could have in there. Teacake will go too, no doubt. I wouldn't have *any* of you go in there alone.' She gives me a hard stare.

Zara glows. 'You see. Humanity has its own power.'

'Humanity has all the power,' Yanny mutters, standing. 'Only not in the forest right now. Come on, then – let's get this over with.'

Zara pulls a face at me. 'Makes him grumpy, being sick.'

'I'm not sick. Just tired.' He pulls his coat on and turns to Nan. 'Thank you, Mrs Brigg, for dinner. It was lovely, but I really must go.' He stalks to the door, but it's laden with charms, and he jolts back when he touches it. 'Stella –' he gestures to the door – 'if you please?'

'Goodness sake,' I say. I pull down the silver bells, unlocking the door and opening it to the brittle, dark night. 'After you. Peg, will you put the bells back up?'

'No, I'll just leave the place unprotected,' Peg says sarcastically.

I glare at him. I've got enough strop on my plate without him joining in.

Teacake scoots out ahead of us, and I give Nan a quick, grateful smile, and she nods with another one of those 'we'll be talking' looks on her face. I blow her a kiss and head out after the others into the wind and the rain, unhitching all the charms around the silver wire so we can get out. Only, they're not live. I forgot to set them again once we were inside.

'Stella?' Peg bounds up to my shoulder. 'Have the barriers been down all this time?'

'No – I just . . .' I stare at him. 'I took them down to let Yanny in, and then I whispered the spell so he'd be able to enter in peace. The silver at the door was working . . .'

'But not the fence.'

'It was only for an hour or so. What do you think might've happened?'

'Probably nothing,' he says. 'Go on. I'll get everything back up. Be safe, Stella. Keep your power close.'

Teacake looks up at him and opens her tiny pink mouth to yowl.

'Yes, that's very reassuring,' he says. 'I'm sure the forest will quail before you, furball.'

A look passes between them that I can't read, and

then she hisses, and bounces off to join Yanny and Zara as they start the trudge towards the dark mass of the forest.

'What was that with Teacake, Peg?' I ask, looking after them. 'Is there anything I should know? How many secrets are you keeping?'

'Oh, many,' he says. 'But as for that little sph—' He chokes, as if he have a furball of his own. 'As for that little kitten, I should say she's exactly what she looks like: silly.'

Centauride/Centaur

Half horse, half human in appearance, powerful, and always on the front line of any conflict in the fae forest realms. Their magic is in the strength they bear, and in the weapons they wield. The bows, swords and daggers forged by their kind are unparalleled in craft or power.

FIGHT – 10	
FLIGHT – 0	
MAGIC – 5	
DISGUISE – 0	

19

The shadows are clustered tight between the trunks of the trees, and they cling to the brittle branches up high, and they crawl through the undergrowth with a sound like the crack of fire. They are shadow imps and shadow cats and shadow wolves, stalking between the giants of shadow men. Yanny takes a breath and strides through as if they don't exist, pulling his faelight from his school bag. Zara follows. And Teacake winds about my ankles. I pick her up and kiss her nose.

'Wait here, if you like,' I say. 'And pull me out, if I get stuck on the way back?'

She puts her face into my neck and purrs, deep and tight, sending waves of warmth through me.

'Thank you,' I say, putting her down.

She walks away a few feet, and then turns back and sits watching us, licking a paw, and I follow the others in, trying not to see the eyes that follow, or to hear the wail of their shadow voices. But the further I go, the closer they get, until my feet have lost the path, and my eyes cannot see past the mist of their forms to my friends. The acorn at my throat is uncomfortably warm, and when I put my fingers to it, there's a snap of static that makes me wince.

'Zara!' I manage.

She is there in an instant, and her warm hand pulls me through, Yanny on the other side. We walk in a chain – Zara in the middle, unseeing, but all too aware of the tension in the air, the warp of the darkness in here.

'No wonder they say it's haunted,' she whispers. 'I've got goosebumps all over!'

'Just . . . keep walking,' says Yanny with an effort.

His faelight is starting to pulse erratically, and I hope he knows where he's going, because I certainly don't. We skirt an enormous yew tree, its twisting roots thick upon the broken ground, and then there's a thunderous echo in the air and a centauride stands before us. She is taller than any man I've ever seen, and her brown hair twists and spirals down her shoulders. Her human torso is painted in the colours of the forest, and her hindquarters are the blue-grey of starless night.

'What are you doing?' she hisses, bending down to Yanny, as Zara and I stare.

'Going home,' Yanny says in a tight voice. 'These are my friends. We're fine.'

'You have the whole of the realm of shadows about you, and the Stag draws near – you are not fine!' she bursts, stamping her hooves. 'You should be more careful, Yanny – your family has lost enough already. Go now, and quickly. I'll divert these creatures.'

She stares at me, her dark eyes blazing. 'I don't know what you are, but you draw the shadows like darkness itself. You are not welcome here. See him home, and be gone, before you stir the rest of the kingdom to rage.' With that, she draws her golden bow and charges into the swathe of shadows, her battle cry sending them spiralling off into the darkness.

'That was Rory,' says Yanny, watching her go. 'I've really made a mess of today. Let's get inside before we cause any more chaos.'

We follow mutely as he treads down the bank to the hidden entrance of his home. Rory's words keep repeating in my mind. She could see straight away the danger I bring here. Does Yanny see it too? Will his family?

Yanny stops at the hatch, looking back at me. 'She has a sharp tongue,' he says, as if he's reading my mind. 'Don't take it personally. She was afraid for us, and fear makes her fierce.' He looks between Zara and me. 'This was my fault. I was the one who got us into trouble. You should head back. Take my faelight . . .'

He thrusts it out, but Zara shakes her head.

'Yanny . . .'

'I know – it's spineless to make you go back on your own. I just can't . . . do any more right now.'

'What did she mean, Yanny?' I ask, knowing I shouldn't; knowing he's already reassured me as much as he can right now. 'About your family having already lost too much?'

'Not now,' he says.

'But I didn't mean to put you in more danger. She said about darkness . . . I'm sorry.'

'Pfft,' says Zara. 'Take no notice of that. *I* see no darkness in you. And besides, Yanny's already explained, she was just cross . . .'

I nod, trying to let her words outplay Rory's, but before we can say goodbye to Yanny, the door swings open behind him, and he topples in with a surprised yelp. His father stands bristling on the doorstep.

'In,' he commands. 'All of you. All the forest is whispering of truant children. I can only imagine it's you, Yanny . . .' He hauls his son up none too gently and starts propelling him down the corridor. The door slams shut behind us, and the quartz in the walls flares. 'Really, this is the last thing we needed. It's enough to get you out to school and back without bringing more trouble.'

Zara and I look at each other as we follow Yanny and his father down the corridor. I guess we're the trouble. My chest feels hollow, my legs like rubber. Nothing ever seems to go the way it should. I can hear Nan telling me to be careful what I wish for, and Peg saying going to school was a really dumb idea. Were they right?

I didn't mean to bring more trouble here.

'Look at this place, Stella!' Zara whispers. 'The roots, and the lights . . . and there are tiny little mushrooms growing in the walls! And flowers!' She grins, clapping her hands together. 'I *knew* there were things I didn't know about – I just *knew* it!'

Her eyes dance, but before I can say anything, we're interrupted.

'Stella,' says Yanny's mum, her expression bright and wild and a little alarming as she darts at us from the kitchen. She takes us both by the wrist and draws us into the warmth. 'Come, we must sort this out. Sit down.'

Yanny is already sitting at the table, and his father is shooing the younger kids into their bedroom. When he turns back from the door, his face is as fierce and fae as hers. The room settles into an amber glow that matches the fire in Yanny's parents' eyes, and Zara and I take seats on the bench by the window, shuffling together.

'This cannot be,' says Elowen. 'Yanny, you are permitted to go to school, and to come home again to us. We do not forbid you friends, but we do forbid you to bring them into danger. And you found danger for yourself when you went out fighting shadows last night without permission. Look at you now. You are lucky Rory was on the prowl.'

'I know,' he says. 'But, Ma—'

'But nothing, son,' she hisses, and her teeth are wolf-sharp, her eyes aflame. 'We will not have this. You take too much upon your shoulders, and it is not wise. What do you think will become of us, should we lose another of you? Do you think we would survive that, Yanny?'

Yanny flinches, but he doesn't say anything.

'You are not to patrol,' Fen says then. 'And you are not to fight, Yanny. That is not your task. It is mine, and your mother's. You may hate to see what it costs us, but that is what you must bear. We all are doing things we would rather not be doing, seeing things we wish we could unsee. This time will pass. There will be brighter days. You will have a future. That is all we ask for you.'

'I want my future here, in the forest,' Yanny says.

'And we hope for that too,' Elowen says. 'Still, you must go to school. And you *must* avoid the shadows.'

Fen sighs. 'I'll make us a hot drink.' He looks across at Zara and me. 'And then we'll see about getting your friends home.'

'Stella – and this is Zara, if I'm not mistaken?' asks Elowen.

Zara can do no more than nod.

'We just wanted to make sure he was safe,' I start. 'I didn't mean to cause trouble . . .'

'Perhaps you didn't,' says Elowen. 'And I am glad my boy has friends, truly. Glad that he is home safe.' She gives us a bleak, pointed smile. 'But if Rory tells you that you draw the shadows, Stella, then she does not lie. You should stay away, for now. And so should Zara.'

'What could the shadows do, though?' Zara asks. 'Won't they just . . . go away?'

'Sadly not.' Elowen sighs. 'I'll leave you to explain the dangers of the shadows, Yanny. Your father and I must get ready for patrol. We will see your friends out on our way.'

'What's going on?' Zara asks later, after Fen has brought steaming mugs to the table and left to get ready. 'Yanny? What is it that you've lost? What's going on here? What is so dangerous about the shadows?'

He wilts a little in his seat.

'I'm sorry,' she whispers. 'I know I ask too many questions. Dad always says—'

'We lost my sister, two years ago,' he says. 'That's what we lost. We lost Thorn.'

'Oh, Yanny,' I manage, shuffling up close to him as Zara does the same on the other side, trying to find words and failing.

'What happened?' asks Zara after a long silence.

'She got ill,' he says. 'We thought it was just a cold, but it got worse so quickly, and nobody could help. By the time we realized it was shadow sickness, it was too late.'

'Shadow sickness?'

'It spreads,' he says. 'It starts in the trees, when they

don't get enough light, and from there it spreads to the fae and the other creatures. Nothing survives without the trees. Thorn loved playing in the canopy. We weren't supposed to because it's hard to tell when a tree is sick from up there. We only noticed it afterwards – and by then, it was too late.'

'Isn't there a cure?'

'No. Sometimes people recover,' he says. 'But when we discovered the tree, it was already dead.' He looks out into the kitchen, but his eyes aren't seeing anything there. 'Dead trees are like poison to fae, especially when they've died because of the shadows,' he says. 'The tree sprites are quick to notice normally, but it was just a young elm, not bonded with any of the sprites. It was already dying when Thorn touched it.' He lifts his shoulders. 'So. Now you know.'

My father's shadows killed his sister.

How would he even look at me if he knew what I really was? If he knew that maybe I could have fixed this years ago, if Nan and I had just kept going . . .

'Stop that,' Yanny snaps at me.

'What?'

'That look. Every time I mention shadows, you get all mournful and sorry. Did you bring them here? Did you make them? Did you send them to kill trees, and young fae?'

My throat is tight with a river of tears, but I swallow them.

'No.'

'So stop it.' He sighs, shoving his shoulder against mine. 'Please.'

'OK,' I say, biting my lip to stop myself from saying sorry again.

Zara looks from him to me, but even she doesn't have the right words. She just shoves herself up closer to Yanny on the other side and tucks her arm through his.

Zara and I hold hands through the forest on the way home, and though we are flanked by Yanny's parents with their faelights, there's a constant shudder down my spine that won't let me rest. I stare into the darkness between the trees, and I stare at the trees themselves for signs they might be sick.

How would I know?

I am fae, and I know barely anything. I don't know what to say to this fierce, bright couple as they stalk soundlessly through the undergrowth, their eyes flecked with amber, every muscle of their bodies ready to strike and defend. To protect us.

'I'm sorry,' I whisper to Elowen, as we reach the edge of the forest.

She looks at me for a long, silent moment, and my breath sticks in my throat. Nan told me the fae were dangerous. I thought she meant wild, and keen to fight, and there is some of that in her – but there is more. There is something so true and stark about her, especially *here*. Her skin gleams beneath the moon, her stance knows the land better than I know anything, her folded wings flicker with bright copper threads, and her stare sees everything.

'I know,' she says. 'Thank you, Stella. Now go – and don't come back until it's time.'

20

'Oh, Stella!' Zara halts as we emerge from the trees, looking back at the forest. 'What is going on? I never saw anything so magical, but that awful sadness . . . And Elowen – what did she mean when she said that to you? Time for what? And what was Yanny going on about, *it's not your fault*. How *could* it be your fault?'

'I don't know,' I say, threading my arm through hers and pulling her back with me, Teacake now tucked under my other arm. 'I don't know what to think about any of it.'

My mind is sparking with too many images, too many ideas of fight and flight and shadow creatures and the monster who is my father, hidden away in there. I always hoped that if I did go in there, if I made it past the shadows to the true fae, that it would be a good thing. That my magic would be stronger, brighter than his; that it would be my mother's moon-sprite power that would shine through. But that didn't happen.

I draw the shadows to me, just as my father does.

'But we *have* to think about it. What do we *do*, Stella?'

I've never seen her so animated. She looks like she might charge back in there and fight the shadows herself if I just said the word. Or run away entirely in the other direction. Her feet are almost stamping with impatience just to do *something*.

'Well?'

'OK. We'll have to make a plan!'

'Yes!' she shouts. 'A plan! Yes!'

I have to go back in there. If I can draw the shadows to me, it must be possible to send them back where they belong. I am the Lost Prince, after all.

A strange high peal of laughter escapes me and rings out through the moorland. Zara stares at me.

'I'm so sorry,' I stutter. 'I know it's not funny. None of this is funny. It's not funny, Zara! We just need to calm down a bit! Stop shouting!'

'You stop shouting!'

'OK!'

And then suddenly it's clear what I have to do next: I have to find him.

I have to find the palace, and I have to find the Shadow King.

I have to take the shadows with me – and make it all stop.

'Children,' says a dark, disapproving voice. Peg flutters down and lands hard on my shoulder. 'What a fine chorus you are making out here in the wild. I've been out here waiting for you. Come, now. Nan has been worried sick, and it's time for Zara to get home before her folks are the same.'

But Zara is staring with horror towards our house, her feet unmoving.

'What is it?' I demand.

She points to the scrubby narrow lane on the other side of the house. A shining silver car has been parked in a hurry, front wheels at an angle. We have a visitor, and it's not Mrs Mandrake – she'd never let go of her ancient once-was-blue truck.

'My mum's here!' she whispers.

21

We trudge through the garden in silence. I cannot imagine what we're going to find inside. Zara hasn't said that much about her mum before – I have no clue how she might handle ghost Nan . . . or Peg, for that matter. Will she just be standing in an empty kitchen? Will Peg be a bird, or a lizard? Will Nan even be there?

'How did she find the house?' I ask.

'Oh, I told her you lived on the edge of the forest. She's probably tried every one,' Zara says. 'I should've sent another text – I forgot.'

'Well come on, then,' I say. 'She's here now; we'd better go in and face the music.'

I push open the back door, wincing as all the bells ring out, and tread lightly into the kitchen, where Nan is pouring tea, a sweet little red bird on one shoulder. A woman with Zara's golden eyes and brown skin sits across from her and looks up as Zara follows me in.

'Ah!' she says. 'Here they are!'

She smiles, but there's worry in her eyes.

'I'm sorry,' begins Zara, fluttering about beside me. 'We were—'

'I've already explained to your mother,' Nan interrupts smoothly, gesturing for us all to take a seat. 'Fishing at twilight is rather special – though I note you didn't catch anything.'

'They weren't biting,' I say, sliding into a chair and plucking a yellow pear out of the fruit bowl. 'I'm sorry we worried you, Mrs Nassar.' I gleam at her, and her eyes soften, though she looks rather bemused. 'The forest is so beautiful, and we lost track of time . . .'

'You both look very cold,' Nan says after a long moment. 'Have some tea . . .' She indicates for me to pour, and my hands are shaking, but I just about manage it without scalding us all.

'It has been a pleasure to meet your nan, Stella. And I'm glad that Zara has found new friends,' says Mrs Nassar. 'But next time, Zara, a little more information, please – and answer your phone! It would have saved me some worry. You have a charming home, Mrs Brigg.'

'Thank you,' says Nan. 'Rather old and dilapidated, much like me, but it serves us well.'

Peg the bird flutters from Nan's shoulder to mine as I reach for a handful of berries, and he pecks at me until I feed him some.

'And such a sweet bird!' Mrs Nassar says. 'Really, the whole place is somewhat enchanting.'

A rather awkward silence falls over the room, until Teacake, who has been sitting in my lap, decides to make a break for the jug of milk, which tips and spills across the table.

'Teacake!' I yelp, grabbing a cloth and swabbing at the milk before it reaches Mrs Nassar.

She jumps up, and after a startled moment watching Peg take flight around the room, while I slap at the table with my cloth, and Teacake scurries around trying to drink as much of the spilled milk as possible, she claps her hands together.

'Time for home, Zara!' she says brightly, picking up her bag.

There is no messing with that voice. Peg lands neatly on the mantelpiece, Teacake sits with her tail wrapped around her paws, a perfect picture of kittenish goodness, and Nan flaps her hands at us with a shake of her head. I note she's getting thin already – it must have taken all her strength to make tea and conversation. I blow her a kiss, and we trail after Mrs Nassar to the front door, calling out our farewells and smoothing down our clothes.

I take a long time saying goodbye to Zara and her mother, but in the end, the car is gone, and I cannot delay the inevitable any longer. It's time to have that talk Nan promised so sternly earlier.

'What a day you've had,' Nan says, just about visible as I settle opposite her, Teacake back on my lap in seconds.

I nod. I don't even know where to start.

'How is Yanny?'

'He's OK. Back at home. Thanks for letting me go—'

'Tell me about it?' she asks, and she looks completely uncertain, in an utterly un-Nan-like way, and not very angry at all, so I do. I don't hold back anything; I just let it all come out. Peg whistles when I get to the end, but Nan doesn't look impressed at all.

'So now you know,' she says eventually. 'You've seen what it's like – what I've been trying to protect you from.'

'But they're all in danger, Nan.'

'And what do you plan on doing about it?' she asks with a sigh.

'I'm going to search for the palace,' I say.

'I thought I had more time,' she says. 'To train you, to teach you of the dangers.'

'All you've ever done is teach me of dangers! What about the good bits? The magic, and the families in there who are helping each other every day?'

'When I returned to care for you, I swore I'd keep you away from the forest until you were grown,' she says, staring into the fire.

'And now I am.'

'So show me.'

'What do you mean?'

'Undo the glamour I put upon you. If you are ready, you'll be able to.'

Her eyes shine in the firelight. Peg watches, and so does Teacake, whom I've placed on the floor beside me. But no matter how deep I dig, what words I mutter, how *much* I want this right now, there is no shift in me. I remember how I glamoured Yanny, and I try to find the edges of what she's done to hide me, but nothing shifts.

Nothing changes at all.

'Nan!' I burst out eventually, stars in my eyes, infuriated with her and all the world.

'There is great power in you, Stella,' she says. 'You

can do this, in time. Your parents and mine were part of the longest period of peace Winterspell has ever known. It was a golden time; we did not know how lucky we were. There was food, and there was laughter. There was the palace, where the fae danced and where nothing was impossible. Many fae forests have disappeared; many destroyed. Many fight for their existence daily . . . ' She shakes her head sadly.

'But our forest is one of the greats; one of the oldest. It was protected by man, and so it thrived. It is still protected, from man's interventions. But what you fight is far wilder. Your father's heart is twisted, and his eyes see only darkness. His shadows have spread through the trees, and you have seen for yourself, they are still destroying the forest now. They take the light, and the energy. They are a curse, and that is why your friend's wings are the way they are. Because of the curse the Shadow King laid upon Winterspell when he retreated into the palace and let his shadow stag run free. You cannot fight that, until you are all that you can be.'

I sit on the bench by the fire. Peg makes more tea in tinkling cups, and Teacake bounces back into my lap again, curling up with a wide, toothy yawn. Nan watches me.

'Rory said I was full of darkness, that I drew the shadows . . .'

Nan is silent for a moment. 'You are not full of darkness. You are the opposite, and that is what attracts the shadows. Whatever we may feel, Stella, there can be no darkness without light, and no light without shade.'

'Why can't he see that? Why does he let this happen, Nan?'

'He is lost,' she says, her voice barely more than a whisper. 'The fae king who was your father is gone, Stella. I am so sorry. I wish it weren't so. I wish I could tell you that you can help him, but you must not go in there hoping for such. When you go in there, it must be with one thought only: to wrest the power from him, to undo the curse, and send the shadows away.'

'How do I do that?'

'I'd tell you, if I knew,' she says.

'I'm going to try, Nan,' I say. 'Even if you think I'm not ready. There must be something I can do. They're all working so hard to survive, and I'm one of them . . .'

'You'll choose your path,' she says. 'I know. I wish it weren't so soon.'

I have so much more to ask her, but her words are faint. She mutters something about patience, but I am not going to just ignore it all now and leave others in danger while I hide in this big old house. My friends need help *now*, not in some fictional legendy future. I stare at Nan, my heart sinking as she slowly fades from view. What can you do when you're living with a ghost? It's impossible to argue with someone who isn't even visible. I don't want to wear her out so much that she disappears for good.

I humph and close my arms around Teacake's warmth, but she struggles against me and drops to the floor, heading upstairs with her tail arrow-straight.

Curious that she'd leave the comfort of my lap, and the warm fire, I look from her to Peg. He's apparently sound asleep, his scales gleaming red-gold as he lies flat out on the mantelpiece.

'Where are you going, kitty?' I whisper, getting up and following her as she heads up the stairs. She glances over her shoulder at me with a small chirrup and walks purposefully down the corridor to the old study.

I follow her inside. It's cold in here, and dark. The heavy curtains are drawn, and there are cobwebs on the ceiling and draping from an old brass chandelier.

'What are we doing in here?' I shiver, taking matches from the desk and stretching up to light the candles in the chandelier. They snap and fizz as the dust burns away, and the flames cast a restless golden light over the room. 'Teacake?'

She gathers herself and launches up on to the bookshelves in the furthest, darkest corner, sending a load of dust swirling into the air. When it settles, she's sitting on the third shelf up.

'OK,' I say. 'That's the shelf, then. What am I going to find? Some tome on the best treats for small cats? A beginner's guide to fishing?'

She swats her tail and narrows her eyes at me, then jumps down and settles on the worn leather chair behind the desk. I look at the shelf: *Ladies of the Fae*; *The Lay of the Land: Protection of Fae Forests*; *Lessons on Blackthorn*; *Love and Lavender: A Text on the Properties of Herbs in Magic*; *The Lost Folk*.

I pull out *The Lost Folk*. It's newer than some of the books here, its cover plain brown with the lettering picked out in copper. The spine creaks as I open it, and some of the pages are uncut. I scoop Teacake up and sit in the warm place she's made, settling her into my lap.

The Lost Folk: Those Who Have Left, and Those Who Long to Return.

It seems to be mostly about extinct fae creatures. It

talks about lost habitats, changes in the air itself. I take the paper knife out of the pot on the desk and carefully break apart the uncut pages. They're handwritten in spiky black lettering. I flick through, my fingers moving over unfamiliar words, until I find it.

Teacake was leading me straight here.

THE LOST PRINCE

When the fae queen succumbed to the Plaga, shadows descended over Winterspell, and great change was wrought. The creatures who had known only peace were slow to realize the danger they were in, but once they saw how the shadows destroyed all they touched, they began to fight. Sometimes, they won, and sometimes they lost. But always, the shadows remained, for the old fae king's mourning knew no bounds, and he hardly knew what he had unleashed upon the world. Hidden in his cursed palace, locked away from all the fae, he saw only his own grief.

The fae will fight for eternity for Winterspell. They need no hero, for they are all heroes living in that magical forest. But there are few who gleam with the moon's own light. And fewer still who can call upon the fae king's heart. The child of the Lost Queen may just be the key, in time.

The Lost Prince will return when he is grown. He will find the palace, though the way is treacherous. He will face his father, and his arrival in Winterspell will herald both a new beginning and an end, in time.

'Oh will it,' I mutter, stroking Teacake. 'What a load of rubbish – it's no help at all. Nan made it up, after all. There is no Lost Prince!'

Teacake makes a questioning sound in the back of her throat, staring hard at me with her unblinking green eyes, and then she sticks her claws into my knee and starts to knead, purring. I tuck the book into my cardigan, and pick her up, heading to my bedroom. What would it have been like to grow up in Winterspell like Yanny did? To be truly part of that fae world? We did live in there, once.

If only I could remember.

22

'Stella!'

Peg pokes his imp head in through the door.

'You didn't say goodnight.'

'You were asleep!'

'That doesn't usually bother you.'

He leaps across the floor and lands on the bed, bouncing Teacake into the air with a fierce little toothy grin. She recovers herself and prowls around him for a moment before curling up next to him, her smoky tail twined with his bright scaled one.

'Pesky creature,' he hisses, but he doesn't move away. 'So, you're not happy?'

'I don't know what to do. Nobody will tell me. They just keep saying *when the time is right* . . . How am I supposed to know when that is? I can't even undo Nan's glamour – I'm useless!

'You are NOT!' he shouts, with a pop of smoke,

rushing over to me. 'Stella, you are *not* useless. You are exactly who you should be. You are brave, and bold, and wilful, and kind – you are the very best of fae!'

'I don't see how that can possibly be true.'

'Perhaps you don't yet,' he concedes, his amber lamp eyes glowing up into mine. 'Just take my word for it. There are other, more pressing things to worry about, if worrying is what you have your heart set on.'

'Like?'

'The fact that you left the boundary unshielded!'

'Not for very long!'

'Shadows are fast,' he says. 'Who knows what they might have heard, or seen.'

'But they couldn't get into the house because of the bells at the door. And we didn't say anything very special, did we?'

'We can only guess what they might have picked up on,' he mutters. 'Something's bothering me though. What if . . .' He stares at the window. 'What if there's still one here . . . in the garden? We could have locked it in by mistake when you sorted the charms out earlier.'

'We should go out and check!' I say, scrambling off the bed.

'That's just what I was thinking,' he says drily, jumping to my shoulder.

'But how do you get rid of a shadow?' I whisper, as we head down the stairs.

'Kill one?'

'No. Send it back to the forest!'

'You don't want to send it back; it'll go running off with all our secrets,' Peg says. 'The trick is for it to *not* go back, Stella.'

'I can't kill something!'

'It isn't a creature, a living thing,' he says. 'It's created out of night itself – a product of fear.'

'Then how do I even *do* anything to it.'

He sniffs. 'I don't know. I've avoided them as much as I can. Perhaps I should have made a study of them instead.'

'Why aren't you allowed in there, Peg?' I ask.

He stares at me for a few moments.

'Not all things can be so easily spoken of,' he says, winding his tail through his fingers. 'It was a misunderstanding. A silly thing that I haven't had the time to fix.'

'So you're not going to tell me?'

'Not now, no,' he says. 'Come on – let's sort this shadow.'

I blow my breath out and shake my head at him, and then we creep through the kitchen, and I shove on my boots and open the back door as quietly as I can, trying not to alert Nan to what we're doing.

The garden is creepy at night. I light the lanterns that swing from iron hooks on the outer stone wall of the house, and the moon is high, but there is still so much darkness. Peg is a sharp-clawed bronze bat on my shoulder, and we dance between the light patches, scouring the empty air for signs of a shadow that shouldn't be there.

'Use your magic,' he hisses after a while. 'That's what attracted them, when you were in the forest. Rory saw it herself. Maybe if you focus on it now, the shadow will be drawn to you.'

'I don't want to draw it to me!' I say. 'And I don't really know what my magic is, Peg. Or how to use it.'

'You've already used it,' he says. 'When you glamoured Yanny, for example, and probably many other times. If you'd just stop telling yourself you can't do it, that might help. Just try,' he says. 'I'm here.'

There's a small howl from my ankles; Teacake has followed us here.

I close my eyes and imagine the magic as a small fire

deep inside me. I picture it getting brighter, filling my veins like a silent stream. When I open my eyes again, my whole body feels like it's on fire.

'Steady,' says Peg.

I breathe out, with a little burst of silver sparks that fizz in the cold air.

'Goodness!' he yelps, scrambling to cover his face with his wings.

'Sorry,' I say.

My tongue feels dry and dusty. I try to calm the rush of energy that's still rolling through me, and that's when I see it. Over by the fence, perched on the henhouse, a small figure with spines running down its back.

'What kind of creature is that?' I ask.

'Could be anything,' Peg whispers. 'They make their forms out of shadow; there are no limits.'

'I suppose that makes sense,' I say. 'In the forest, there were wolves, and birds . . . and the Stag . . .'

The creature looks back over its shoulder at us, and hisses, revealing iron-grey teeth that shine.

'It doesn't seem to be attracted,' I say.

'Give it a minute.'

I focus on steadying the energy, until it's a low hum. The creature jumps down from the henhouse and hunkers low on the ground, barely visible, and after what seems an age, it starts to move towards us.

'What do I do?' I whisper, terrified.

Teacake stretches out on the ground before my feet and rolls on to her back, exposing her tiny belly, the picture of unconcern. I frown.

'Silly kitten,' growls Peg. 'What's she doing?'

'Something,' I say.

I crouch down, put a hand on her pale fur. She curls up around my hand, her claws sharp against my skin, but not digging in, her green eyes staring as if she's trying to tell me something. The shadow edges ever closer, watching intently, but I act like I don't care. Like this is all perfectly normal. And then, when it's crept closer than my mind can really bear, and all my skin is goosebumps, I take my hand away from Teacake and curl my fingers around my acorn, turning to face the shadow.

'Go, Stella!' says a little voice in my mind.

And so I do, eye to eye, fear against fear, I howl. A little bright spark flares around me, and the shadow is, after all, just a shadow, I tell myself in a hard, new voice. In this garden, in my home, it does not have the power of many – no power over me. The sparks keep flying, and the shadow unravels, and then I'm breathing hard, and Teacake is sitting pert and watchful, and Peg is his beautiful imp self, his tail curling over my shoulders, and the garden is, just for an instant, a blaze of pale light.

'That'll do it!' Peg claps his hands. 'Yes, Stella!'

I don't really know whether it was me, or Teacake, or some kind of team effort, but the shadow is gone, and hopefully with it, any secrets it might have learned.

I turn and head back into the kitchen with Teacake tucked under one arm, and Peg perched on the other, and we drink warm milk huddled together on the old settee, staring into the still-glowing embers of the fire for a bit. It's warm, and they keep close, and there is so much to think about, but I am restless, because I did it. I sent a shadow away, and if I can do that to one, I should be able to do it to many.

I should be able to do it in Winterspell.

23

School is weird the next day. From the moment I get in, the sense of everything is different. The magical kids look at me suspiciously, and without Yanny, it feels far less friendly.

'You're causing trouble,' says Tash, as soon as I sit down. 'I can't believe you let a human up here. Haven't you read the contract?'

'I have, thank you. And if *you* have, you'll know there are exceptions. Besides, you were the one who left the door open!'

She freezes, as everyone turns to watch us.

'So, I don't think anyone else has a problem with her coming in,' I continue. 'She's our friend, so she stayed to help Yanny. She looked after him better than you have.'

'What would you know about that?'

'Well, where were you? When he was struggling with his glamour, I didn't see you hanging about to help!'

'I have my own glamouring to see to,' she says. 'I haven't got enough for anybody else. You're lucky you don't need to do it. What are you, exactly?'

'I'm a sprite,' I say sharply, staring at her. She's a moon sprite herself – I remember Yanny saying. Perhaps that accounts for her silver eyes and the night-dark hair that spirals around her face.

'I thought you looked a bit crinkly about the hairline!' says a small, round-limbed girl called Wren, coming over to sit next to me. She has tiny, beautiful horns at the top of her forehead. 'Look – your ears are just the *tiniest* bit pointed, like mine.' She pulls back her shining brown hair to reveal her own pointed ears, and grins. 'Welcome, Stella – sprite girl.'

'Thank you, Wren,' I say, looking between her and Tash. 'I didn't mean to cause trouble. I just wanted to come to school. I didn't realize there would be fae here.'

'And you live in that funny old house?' Wren asks, while Tash glowers at us both. 'Who with?'

'My nan, and Peg, and Teacake.'

'What's a peg? Who's Teacake?'

'Teacake is a cat. And Peg's an imp.'

'An imp! Your family must be important for him to

stick around. They don't like staying in one place much.'

'I think he just likes Nan.'

'Who's *Nan*?' asks Tash.

'My grandma. She's a ghost.'

There's a stunned silence.

'You mean . . . ghosts are real?' whispers Wren. 'Like, she talks and everything? Can she move things? Is she bound to your house? Ooh! Could you bring her to school?'

I stifle a laugh at the thought of bringing Nan to school.

'You didn't know that ghosts were real?' I ask.

'We *still* don't know they're real,' says Tash.

'No!' says Wren. 'My parents always said they were legends; just stories told to children to teach them lessons about things.'

'Well, humans do that about the fae,' I say.

Wren laughs, but Tash sniffs and looks at her long, pointed nails. I bite my lip to stop myself from saying anything else stupid.

'Don't worry about Tash,' says Wren. 'She's not great with new people. She's not great with old people either, to be honest – but she does get easier with time.'

Tash stalks off and gets into a fierce debate with

someone on the other side of the room, gesticulating out of the window.

'What's that about?' I ask.

'It was a bad night in the forest,' Wren says. 'Something's shifted, and nobody really knows why. No disasters, exactly, but the nights are so long now that it's winter, and even the daylight is just murk. The ivy on the trees has grown so thick, it hardly lets any light through. More of them are getting sick.'

'Is Yanny OK?'

'Strictly under house arrest,' she says. 'And I don't expect he's happy about it!'

'It was my fault.'

'It wasn't.' She frowns. 'From what I heard, you just made sure he got home safe. I heard you dealt with the shadows pretty well yourself . . .'

I sigh. 'I don't know about that.'

'But we know you have some affinity with the shadows – Rory told us.' says Tash, 'which seems pretty strange to me.'

The room instantly feels darker and colder. Wren rolls her eyes and tries to brush it aside, and Principal Ashworth comes in and starts waffling about Safety in the Modern Human World, but the feeling stays, and it isn't only Tash who looks sideways at me after that. It's a huge relief to get out of there and downstairs, where Zara is waiting for me.

'Why does everyone look so glum?' she whispers, tucking her arm through mine and leading me off to tutorial.

'It was a difficult night in the forest, apparently,' I say. 'And they all think I'm some kind of evil shadow-bending sprite creature, so that didn't really help.'

'A what?'

'Something Tash said . . .' And Rory, whose coldness I can't forget. The way the shadow drew close to me last night, before I sent it away.

'Don't listen to her,' Zara says. 'There's nothing evil about you. Speaking of which, I wondered . . . Mum's working a late shift tonight – maybe I could come to yours?'

I grin at her. 'You just want to see Peg again!'

'He is amazing,' she says. 'But also, I figured . . . maybe it's a bit lonely sometimes at yours. I know it's lonely at mine when Mum's at work.'

'Doesn't anyone stay with you?' I ask.

'My aunt comes and stays if Mum's working nights,

but late shifts mean she's home by nine, so I sort myself out.'

'What about . . . Do you see your dad much?'

'Not so much,' she says, marching on through all the kids, dragging me with her. 'Anyway. Tea tonight? We need to work out a plan, anyway, right?'

'Definitely! But . . . Zara.'

She turns back to me.

'You can talk to me, if you want to . . . about things. You know that?'

'I know,' she says with a wobbly sort of smile. She takes a breath. 'It's complicated.'

I nod. 'But when you're ready.'

'When I'm ready, you'll be the first to know,' she says. 'Come on. We'll be late.'

I pull her close as we walk, just so she knows she isn't alone. Even if sometimes she feels that way.

24

'All right?' asks Zara, frowning as I fumble with the charms at the gate.

My head started buzzing on the way home, and my vision is full of sparking lines.

'Yeah. I don't know. Got a bit of a funny head.'

'It's been a full-on couple of days,' she says.

'I guess.'

I get the charms out of the way, and then replace them over the wood as we close the gate behind us, muttering a few words. It makes my head throb.

'Come on,' says Zara. 'Let's get you inside.'

She takes the key from my hand, letting us both into the warm kitchen, where Nan and Peg are already entertaining. Yanny looks up from an enormous cheese sandwich with a grin that doesn't quite meet his eyes.

'Hey.' He waves.

'Stella?' Nan knows straight away there's something amiss. 'What's wrong?'

'Just a headache,' I say.

It's already easing, I realize, as I drop my bag and throw off my coat. Zara takes it from me and hangs it with hers on the pegs by the door, and Peg puts the kettle on.

'How was school?' Yanny asks around a mouthful of sandwich.

'Oh, OK,' I say, dropping into a chair. 'I thought you were under house arrest.'

'Well . . . no. A bit. I said I was coming here. They weren't exactly thrilled about it, but I think they knew they weren't going to stop me.'

'You can help us with our studies,' says Zara.

Yanny looks curious, and I stare at Zara, hoping she's not going to say much more in front of Nan.

'Do you have homework?' Nan asks. 'I have heard of that.' She looks very proud of the fact, sitting by the fire with Teacake on the arm of her chair.

'Yes. History. We were going to do it in the study.'

'Good idea,' she says. 'About time that room got used for some actual studying. Might be dusty though –

you'll need to take a cloth. There's an old feather duster somewhere . . .'

We sit and have tea with her first, and though I can see it's tiring for her, she's bright with chatter, happy to tell Zara some of her stories.

Peg sees us upstairs after tea, once Nan has drifted off. He swishes the feather duster with his tail as we go, and Teacake follows behind.

'What's this studying all about then?' Yanny demands once we're in the wood-panelled room.

'Just looking into things,' I say, making my voice casual. 'We have all these books; they may be useful. That's all.'

He nods, but he doesn't look very happy about it. 'Dad would love it in here,' he says, prowling around the shelves. 'He loves old books.'

'So does Peg,' I say. 'I just thought we'd see what we can find. I want to shift this glamour spell of Nan's, and then I'm going to go back into the forest to find the palace.'

'Isn't that dangerous?' asks Zara.

'For most people, it would be,' Yanny says, sitting on the bench by the window, looking out towards Winterspell. 'Not for our Stella, though.'

'What do you mean?' Zara asks.

I can't speak; my mouth is dry. He already knows.

'Stella is the Lost Prince,' Yanny says. 'And she isn't going to find her answers in any of these old books.'

'Yanny!'

'Well?' he demands, his eyes glinting. 'Tell me you aren't the Lost Prince. Swear it.'

'I . . . can't.'

Zara frowns. 'You're what? What's this about a Lost Prince? What have I missed now?'

'It's a legend,' Yanny says. 'He is the child of the old fae queen and the king we now call the Shadow King. The Lost Prince was taken from the forest, and will return one day – and when he returns, everything will change in there. *He* is a symbol of hope.' He stares at me.

'Nan made it up,' I whisper, swallowing hard. 'I mean, you're right. I am the Shadow King's daughter.' I feel my skin flushing, and the acorn at my throat is warm. 'I found my mother's acorn, that first time I came into Winterspell with you, and since then, my magic has been growing. I think that maybe I can help, but I need to know how to get rid of this glamour Nan did so that I can fight, so that I can find the palace—'

'You already have everything you need!' Steam drifts from Yanny's mouth as he speaks. 'You're just wasting time, Stella!'

'That's harsh, Yanny,' says Zara with a hard look. 'You don't need to shout about it. Stella's not responsible for everything that happened – she's trying to help!'

'Not quickly enough,' he says. 'While she's in here all safe and cosy, trees are dying in Winterspell – and you both know what that means!' His eyes glitter as he stares at me, and I know we're all thinking about Thorn. About all he's lost already. 'You are the Lost Prince, Stella. Don't you see that? Even if your nan made up the legend, she made it up about *you*. So you're the Lost Princess, instead – who cares what the title is! *You're* still the one who could make the difference.'

'You're right,' I say reluctantly, remembering how I was able to get rid of the shadow last night. There's no more time for waiting; I need to see if I can do the same in Winterspell. I need to get past the shadows to the palace. 'I should've done more, sooner,' I say, feeling wretched.

'But what?' Zara demands. 'You have to have a plan before you go flouncing off in there!' 'No matter who she is, Lost Prince or not, she's still just one small person,

Yanny! You can't just rush in and save everything, even if you really want to. You have to think about how – and you have to work together . . .' she looks between us hopelessly. 'We all have to work together, don't we? Isn't that what this is all about? Sticking together, no matter what? Nobody's got it easy; *everybody's* fighting. Even if it doesn't look like it, even if everything is quiet on the surface, everyone's got a war going on somewhere. Do we all have to shine like the moon just so that you can see when something hurts? *Nobody* knows what they're doing – we're all just trying our best. And we should be doing that together, not keeping secrets and blaming each other!'

Her eyes are bright with unspilt tears, and I don't know what to say. What do I know of how her life has fallen apart with her parents' separation? How have I helped her?

'I'm sorry,' I say.

'Stop being flipping sorry about everything!' she howls. 'Just be you!' She stares between us both, and her eyes are just as fiery – just as stormy – as I've ever seen in any fae.

'So when are you going to do this saving of us all?' Yanny asks a few moments later. 'I suppose in the depths of night, when the shadows are at their strongest, and the moon is a crescent in the sky, and all the bells are ringing?'

'Don't be silly,' growls Peg, making us all jump. 'We'll do it at dawn. When the centauride calls. That's the time to do it.'

'We?' I ask.

'Just you try stealing off alone,' he says, his scales flashing as he rounds on me, eyes ablaze. 'See where that gets you.'

Teacake jumps off the shelf and sits by him, her chest puffed, so they seem in agreement about that, if little else.

'But I don't want to put any of you in danger.'

'It isn't up to you,' Zara says with a sweet, steely smile. 'It isn't only your fight. And you aren't the only one who feels it.'

'I didn't mean . . .'

'Sure you didn't.' Yanny sighs. 'It's a sprite thing. Superior – always have been. I'll leave you to your studies – I have to get back. Some of us can't be waiting around for their magic to just *happen*.' He twiddles his fingers in a mock-mystical sort of way.

'I'm not just waiting!' I protest. 'I promise—'

'Stop reacting to him!' Zara snaps. 'He's being an idiot. And so are you, frankly. You're both too pig-headed to sort this out, and I'm not hanging around while you two carry on shouting at each other.' She grabs her bag and bolts out before I can say anything.

Yanny stares at the place where she was. 'Her parents rowed,' he says, wincing as the kitchen door slams down below us.

I shake my head. 'I should have stopped her from going . . .'

'She probably needs some time out from all this,' Yanny says, his eyes flashing. 'I know I do.'

And he too turns and marches out of the door.

'Oh, Peg,' I say into the new silence. 'That wasn't very good, was it?'

Teacake gives a chirp as I sit down on the bench below the window and bounces into his usual spot in my lap.

'It's what happens,' Peg says, 'when people care about each other, and times are difficult.'

'Should I go after them? I don't know what to do!'

'Let it be for tonight,' he says. 'And in the morning, everything will feel different – it always does. We can fix it.'

'Can we, Peg?' I ask, my voice wobbling. He flings over to me, perching on the windowsill and looking me right in the eye. 'Can we really? Because I want to go in there and find that palace, and make everything better, but I seem to be doing it all wrong already!'

'*I* don't think so,' he says slowly, still staring at me. 'I can see adventures. All you need to work out, Stella, is whether you're ready. If you're ready, all the rest will fall into place.'

25

In the morning, it doesn't feel like the sort of day for an adventure to happen. It feels like a staying in and reading sort of day. Cold, brittle rain splashes against the windows, and it's so dark, I can't even make out the silver wire fence. Nan watches silently as I force a piece of toast down my throat, and Peg whisks up a hot chocolate that burns my mouth and makes my eyes ache.

For so long, this has been us: my family, my home. And it's safe, and warm – and out there, it's wild and wet, and my friends are hurting, and shadows are spreading, and I know I'm going to go in there today, and I'm going to fight with all that I have to find that palace, but I *still* don't have the slightest clue how to make any of it better.

It was a night of tossing and turning. My stomach tight; eyes aching from crying; all the conversations of the day rushing through my head. Teacake stayed rumbling beside me for all of it, at one point rubbing her face into mine, drying the tears. I kissed her and thanked her, mainly because it was her hunting time, and she'd stayed in for me.

She's out there now.

They're all out there. While I stay in here, with my hot chocolate and my watchful nan.

I pick up the crockery and drop it into the sink with a clatter.

'I'm going in now,' I say into the silence.

'I know I can't stop you,' Nan says. And if ghosts can cry, then she is, though it doesn't show on her face. 'But you're still under the glamour, Stella. You haven't got all of your power yet.'

'It doesn't matter,' I say. 'I have *some* power, and that will have to be enough. My friends are in there, and they know who I am. That legend of yours about the Lost Prince is still spoken about, and even if they don't all believe it, it still means something. It means *me*. I wish we'd helped sooner.'

'I know,' she says. 'Honestly, Stella, if I thought we could have, then I would. They are my folk in there, as much as they are yours.'

'And yet we left them.'

'I died!' she says. 'It was my time. And then, when I

returned, it was as *this* flimsy thing. Your mother used the last of her magic to bring me back; it was her last wish that I be here to care for you. And energy is finite, Stella. I had to make sure I'd be around for as long as you needed me. I realized that day when we were on the edge of Winterspell, and the shadows rushed around us, that I didn't have the strength to fight them *and* to look after you . . . I chose you.' She leaves her chair and comes towards me, her figure pulsing. 'I would always, will always – I shall *never* regret choosing you.'

She cups her hands around my chin, and though they don't touch me, I can feel the warmth there.

She has always been here. A bit faded, a bit tattered, sometimes downright see-through. But always, always here.

'OK,' I say finally, when I can find my voice again.

She moves away, settling back into her chair.

'So, I'll do it for the both of us.'

She smiles through the worry in her eyes. 'Don't lose your way,' she says, her voice clear and firm, regal. 'Keep to the path. Find the palace. And when you get there, keep going. Find what you need in there and break the curse – blast those shadows to smithereens. And when you've done that, my Stella, you'll see Winterspell just as it always was. Just as it should be once more. Peg, find the lantern! You'll go with her this time.'

'I know I will.' He sighs. 'Even though technically I'm banished . . .'

'That isn't going to stop you now, my warrior Peg.'

He bristles and then starts digging around in the cupboard by the back door, finally dragging out an old, dusty lantern with glass sides and stiff metal shutters.

'Behold, the oldest fae lamp in all the world, with a crack that surely shall lead to our downfall,' he says miserably, blowing at it and coughing on the dust.

'We'll be fine,' I say, grabbing it from him and giving it a wipe with a tea towel.

It begins to glow, and so I take a deep breath, straighten my spine, grab my coat from the brass hook and march out of the back door without a backward look – straight into Zara.

'Hey!' She staggers back. 'Steady, with your swinging lantern and all! What are you doing?'

'Zara!' I clatter her into an awkward hug, not sure I've ever been so glad to see anyone. 'You came back!'

'Well, I wasn't about to let you have an adventure on your own,' she says. 'I mean . . . if I can come, that is. I'm sorry I dashed off like that . . .' She draws back, and for the first time, I can see the doubt in her. She's been so invested in everything, and it must be hard. Being in a new town after her parents' separation, making friends with people who turn out to not be people at all.

'Please come,' I say. 'I don't know what I'm doing, and this lantern is a bit broken, and Peg's supposed to be coming, but he's still HIDING in the house, and *I'm* sorry. I'm so sorry that we got into a row like that. I didn't mean to keep secrets from you. The whole Lost Prince legend is so messed up.'

'You *are* the Lost Prince, though,' she says.

'I'm the Shadow King's daughter,' I say. 'So, whatever the legends say, I guess that must mean something. Yanny was right. It *is* me. I was panicking – I didn't know what to do. Peg said it would all look different in the morning.' I look around at the slowly brightening sky. 'I suppose it does. Are you OK?'

'I am.' She smiles. 'And it's OK. I've got my own secrets.'

'You have? What are they?'

'Ha! As if I'd tell you so easily. You'll have to wait and see!'

'OK. But whatever they are, it won't change anything. I already think you're awesome, you know.' I grin.

'Of course I know,' she says, tucking her arm through mine. 'The feeling is mutual, Stella. Whoever you are.'

'PEG!' I shout, as we go through the gate and out on to the moors. 'Come on!'

He joins us a moment later, scuttling over scrubby grass beneath a shift of fog, which hangs below a star-bright, lightening sky. Teacake bounds out of Winterspell towards us and gives a little yowl of approval.

My breath steams, and my nerves start to kick in, like little shocks under my skin. The shadows instantly gather, thick at the edge of the forest, and we form a little chain: Teacake at the front, her fur on end; then me, with imp Peg on my shoulder; and Zara at the back, clutching my hand.

Her skin is warm, and the heels of our hands fit together like I never knew could happen. All those times I wanted a real, solid hand to hold, now I have one, and I'm leading its owner straight into danger. She tightens her fingers in mine, stronger than they look, and when I look back, she's bright with the adventure of it all, her eyes gleaming.

And then the horn sounds. A golden ripple that takes our breath away and bursts through the shadows, just for an instant, as Rory calls the new day, and the trees shift, the birds lifting in flight.

We venture in, through the narrow path that twitches at every corner with creatures awakening. As the horn fades, the shadows creep back in, and they come thick and fast, unfurling in the winter air. I'm turned around so quick, that before I know it, Zara is leading the way, Peg barking out instructions I can barely hear through the growl of the wolves and the screech of the shadow birds that loom down from outstretched, blackened branches, their forms twisted and elongated.

'Focus!' Peg snaps at me. 'Can't leave your friend to do this alone. Now is the time, Stella.'

I take a long, deep breath, put my fingers on the silver-and-gold acorn, and keep my eyes trained on Zara. The shadows retreat to the corners of my eyes, and I watch as Teacake darts back and forth before us as if she's testing out the ground – perhaps she is.

Peg digs his claws into my shoulder, and we keep going until the path widens, and daylight streams into the clearing around the wildest part of the river, where the shadows are afraid to roam. They still flick and whisper through the branches of the trees, but in this space, there is clear air, and the rush of silver water sounds like hope.

Teacake halts here and stares up at me, as if waiting for me to act.

'Where's the palace, Peg?' I whisper.

'I don't know where it is,' he says. 'That's the whole point, Stella. Nobody does. Nobody has been able to find it, all this time. I did try, before I was banished . . .'

'You never did say why – perhaps now is the time? Who banished you? The shadows?'

He huffs, letting out a sulphurous cloud. 'Not them. No. The head of the council, Rory.'

'The centauride,' whispers Zara, her eyes round. 'She banished you? Oh dear.'

'Why *oh dear*?' I ask. 'I know she's fierce, but . . .'

'I read about her in one of your books. She's the head of the fae.'

'But the king and queen—'

'No. Well. Yes, they ruled. But after the shadows came, the council was formed to fight them and to rule Winterspell . . . They're the ones with the real power now. They protect the fae people against the shadows, as much as they can.'

'What book did you find that in?' I ask.

'Well,' says Zara, 'I also talked to someone who knows about it all—'

'Anyway,' says Peg. 'Yes, it was Rory who banished me, but she was angry at the time. Perhaps she's forgotten—'

Laughter rings through the clearing, and the flowers that nestle in between the roots of the ancient trees bloom blue and yellow and violet. And Rory is there. She moves towards us, and the air gets thin, and her dark eyes spark.

'*Forgotten?*' she chimes. 'When I make a rule, it is not *forgotten*, Peg. It is not *broken*! You were told never to come back! That spell you used last time nearly destroyed a whole cluster!'

'A cluster?' I frown from Rory to Peg. 'A cluster of what?'

'Spiders,' Peg says, winding his tail through his fingers, looking at the ground. 'I was searching for the truth, deep in the forest, looking for the palace, and they attacked . . .'

'Peg! You were searching for *chestnuts*, and the spiders spooked you. We do not harm nature's creatures in here, even if we don't like them. What you did was unforgivable.'

'I'm very sorry,' he says, looking up at her with a nervous, toothy imp smile. 'I acted wrongly in a moment of panic, and I have repented ever since. I swear, I'll never do it again. Now I bring these children to you, for they are determined to find the palace.'

Rory snorts and paws at the ground. 'Pretty words, little imp – that's all those are.' She turns her steely gaze to me. 'I told these girls, this *creature*, not to return. I told *you* not to return!'

'She isn't a *creature*,' says Peg quickly, leaping up on to my shoulder. 'Don't you see who she is, Rory? Have you been blinded by all these years among the shadows?'

'I have been too busy fighting to listen to dusty old legends,' she whispers, and her face is changed; it is a wild, cruel place where hope no longer lives. 'If what you say is true, then they will find their way, Peg. But you may *not* go with them.'

She is suddenly still, just inches from us. The air smells of metal, it's cold as a knife in my throat.

'You were banished by my word, and my word shall have power here, whatever else may happen. Send your girls to do their little hunt, if you dare. That one –' she indicates me with a cool nod of her head – 'brings the shadows close. There is no doubting that. They have grown worse than ever since I first saw her in here. If she really has something to do with it all, she may as well do it now, for we are heading for the fight of our lives.'

She casts a glance towards Zara and me. 'I see they have one of the old lanterns. Perhaps that will help. Perhaps not. In either case, I have other things to attend to, for today we mourn, for the thousandth time.' The knife sharpens as her voice breaks, and she is grief, and wilderness, all trapped in sharp angles.

Peg crouches still as stone upon my shoulder, and I sense something passing between Rory and him. The moment stretches, and I can almost hear it, but every time I try to tune in, something snaps, tight as elastic. I close my eyes to focus better, but the air turns still . . . and when I open them, she's gone.

'What was that, Peg?'

'A warning,' he says, sounding tired. 'I cannot go with you. And if you don't do this now, you may never get in here again. Rory will see to that.'

He gives me a long, level look, and then starts barking out instructions, about silent mushrooms and the creep of the wilder-vine, and there's something about the shadows, and the yew . . . but I can't concentrate. All my reason is unravelling in here.

Zara looks how I feel. She stares at Peg while he explains everything, and when he's done, she nods, but I don't think she knows any better than I do quite what he was saying. He lifts from my shoulder with one last, sharp warning to keep the lantern fully lit, and takes to the air on red-gold wings. Teacake sticks close beside us and chirrups, and on we go, through the tangle of wood, past the silent ranks of golden ash and the sharp, winter shadows that make our breath bloom like smoke.

For a moment, all things seem possible. The air is clear and quiet; the shadows hardly more than mist—

And then they are among us – a choking, fighting whirl of darkness, which takes my spirit and drives me to my knees, while Zara screams.

26

I can't see.

I can't breathe.

All I can hear is the silence that rings hollow after Zara's scream. I get to my feet slowly, and all my chest is cramped and tight, and the shadows swarm around me.

'Zara?' My voice is a whisper. 'Zara!'

'I'm here,' she says. 'Is that the shadows, Stella? I can't see them, but I think I can feel them – it's *horrible*. I feel so hopeless, like my heart is breaking . . . I thought I knew what that felt like, but maybe I didn't . . .'

I move towards her voice, but the shadows are stronger. They form into their wolf selves, and their teeth glint against the darkness.

'Get away from me,' I hiss, stretching my hands out to feel for her, silver sparks breaking the air.

They hiss back, snakes in the frozen grass between the trees.

'Zara, keep talking!'

'I thought when we moved here, and Dad stayed behind, and I cried so much that my throat hurt . . . I thought that was what it felt like. But here, it feels like something's got its hand around my heart. And I keep seeing his face as we drove off. And I wanted Mum to turn around, but she just kept driving, and her knuckles were all tight on the steering wheel. I knew she was just as torn apart as he was, and we'd done all the talking and all the packing, so I *knew* we weren't just going to turn around, but I was so angry, I didn't care.'

She's silent for a moment, and then her voice comes again, softer now.

'I didn't want to come here,' she says. 'I didn't want a new start. I didn't want to be away from him. I didn't want to see my Mamani crying. And people said they were wrong to separate, because they'd made a promise . . . but they rowed so much. And even when they weren't rowing, they were sad. And now they're not. Or they are, but not so much. Dad laughed, when we went bowling, because we were so rubbish at it, and I realized I hadn't seen him laugh for so long. And Mum . . . I mean, it's not easy, but she doesn't look so . . . *pinched*. She has new friends. That has to be a good thing. Doesn't it?'

I keep going, towards her voice.

'It sounds like a good thing,' I manage through gritted teeth, using the lantern to batter at the flanks of the wolves; steeling my shoulders against the wings of the shadow owls. 'New friends are a good thing.'

Finally I see her, head down, eyes closed, her back against a broad oak tree, and I reach out through the shadows to grab her arm. She turns to me, wild-eyed, and gives me a great big wobbly smile, as I pull her in and hold her close.

'It's OK,' I say, and she laughs, because we're about as far from OK as we could be, lost in this cursed forest. 'We just need to keep going.'

'You know you're glowing,' she says, pulling back after a moment.

'Like moonshine?'

'Yes!'

'Good,' I say. 'That's got to count for something.'

'What are you doing?' says a familiar voice, as a thin faelight cuts a new path through the shadows.

Yanny, his hair standing on end, smoke licking at the ground by his feet, eyes on fire. His fiery whip curls from his wrist and flickers with amber flames. Yanny in warrior mode. Utterly wild and looking very cross.

'I'm going to the palace,' I tell him.

'Good . . .' He hesitates. 'Have you thought about what you'll do? What he'll be like?'

'Not too much,' I say. 'I know what he's like. I know what he was before my mother died. And I know what he is now.' I don't know how to explain what I'm going to do; I don't even understand it myself. But I know there is power here, inside me, and in the acorn that pulls me onward. 'You'll just have to trust me.'

He looks so conflicted, but there's no time for more talk – the shadows are coming thicker and faster, and it's all we can do to keep parrying them with his whip and my lantern. If we don't do something now, they're going to consume us all.

'Go, then,' he says, his eyes flicking up at Teacake. 'You've got your army with you – I'll stay here and watch your back.'

I nod. 'Where are all the others?'

'They're on their way,' he says. 'We've done this before. You go – break the curse, and all this will be over. Don't worry about me.' He gives a wicked, glittering smile, and my heart pounds as I return it.

'Be careful, Yanny,' says Zara, and she sounds as afraid for him as I feel. He's just a slight, bright thing against so much darkness.

He winks, and the shadows come between us, and I put my fingers on to the acorn at my neck, just to check, and there it is, shining at me through a sudden opening in the trees – a swathe of ice as barren as my father's heart.

I stumble on the wiry roots and slam my way through the bracken, fighting as much as running, fending off the brittle twigs that claw at my clothes, Zara by my side.

How could we leave him on his own?

I keep twisting through the trees, knowing that if I stop for even an instant, I'm going to turn back around and tell him we were wrong, there's nothing we can do better than fight by his side. But the way gets colder as we go, and I know we're getting closer to what Nan and I sought, so many times, except we never got this far. We didn't fight through the clinging, fractal ice spider webs that splinter now against my cheeks and snap against the outthrust palms of my hands. We didn't see them.

Zara is quiet as I pull her behind me. Teacake shifts on my shoulder as I turn back, and her breath is coming in great plumes of steam, her eyes wide, lashes coated in fine feathers of ice.

'You're sure about this?' I ask, because Zara is brave, and she's far more than I ever imagined a friend could be, but she cannot feel the thrum of the acorn on the copper chain beneath my shirt; she does not fight for a family she only barely remembers. For a forest full of magical creatures.

She fights for me, and for Yanny.

She digs the heel of her hand into mine, and she doesn't speak, but she sets her chin and nods, and we forge onward together, and it gets colder still as we go, and then there's a row of tall, slender silver birches before us, gathered tight, branches interwoven. We tread around the outside, but there's no break between them. Their roots are glinting arcs of ice, with limbs tightly laced, and their shadows already alive, boiling across the frozen ground. Tiny creatures nestle up high in the glittering canopy, looking down with large, unblinking eyes. Bats, and squirrels, and stoats – all dark-eyed and white-furred.

His creatures.

He will know we're coming.

The shadows are waiting.

'So much for stealth,' I whisper.

Zara shrugs. 'Stealth is overrated. What we need to do is burst through roaring.'

'Really?' I shiver at the thought, but Teacake yowls on my shoulder with a furry, feline sort of a nod.

Zara shrugs. 'What've we got to lose?'

I stare at her. '*Ourselves!*'

'We're already lost.' She grins. 'You've been lost for a lifetime, Stella. You're *famous* for it, remember!'

I stare up at the twisted branches of the trees, willing for a parting, for the slightest gap. We don't have time to linger, while Yanny fights alone. One step down into the packed snow, four inches deep and creaking like old wood. Teacake drops from my shoulder and prowls ahead, and the trees stand like white-bearded silver sentries, shoulder to shoulder.

'I'm coming,' I warn them, my heart catching at the thought of hacking through those gathered branches. The acorn grows warm at my neck, and a tiny flash breaks through the winter air. 'I need to get into the palace, so I'm going to run, and we're going to fight you until we're through . . . unless you get out of my way.'

One more step.

The trees do not part – if anything, they seem to bunch tighter, lowering their crowned heads. The white-furred weasels scramble into their hiding places, and there's a deep, resounding boom, a great rumble deep down below us. We stagger, my knees are shaking, my head is full of shadow and fear, and then a great tide of snow and ice breaks from the tangle before us, rising up before plummeting down to the ground in a mist of cold so deep and thick that it rushes into our eyes and our mouths and throws us down.

Teacake bounces up first, her coat streaks of snow and shadow; she is hardly more than a blur of pink nose and green eyes. She pounces on us, her silver claws like needles, and she doesn't stop until we've scrambled up, wincing and complaining.

This is hopeless . . .

Except, when I can see again, I realize perhaps it isn't.

It is still winter here, and the land is thick with shadow, but the trees are only limed with frost now – they aren't clogged with it. There are spaces between their trunks. They've cleared the way.

I look at Zara. She braces herself, as I do the same, and then we run straight through those gleaming silver trees, and they lift their arms up high so that not a single twig touches us as we go, and the acorn around my neck bursts into golden light, and there is no shadow made in the world that I will not fight to finish this.

27

The palace has been hidden for a decade, ever since my mother died, and my nan made her spell to keep me safe; ever since anyone saw my father. It rises up before us now, and takes my breath away. It's a colossal, marble tangle of sweeping outer staircases, roof gardens where ice apple trees grow, and turrets topped with needle-sharp twists of green copper. Gargoyles spout rivulets of ice down over snow-encrusted window ledges, and great sheets of glittering frost cover every doorway.

And in every dark space, between every crenellation, lurking along the very edges of the palace, are yet more shadows. They are snarling foxes, dark-eyed hares, and other spiny creatures I cannot name. They gather, darker and faster, until the air is as thick as it is cold. But they do not strike. They do not move towards us.

'Do you really think he's here?' I whisper, as Teacake

bounds before us, half disappearing into the snow with every landing.

W NTE PELL, reads the twisted silver sign over the main gate, its bars jagged with splintered ice.

'*Something's* here,' Zara replies, making my spine itch.

'I'm not ready,' I say, halting in my tracks.

'Yes you are.'

'Zara—'

'Stella!' she rounds on me, and her face is fierce, her eyes glowing. 'This is it! And I do love you for all the thinking you do, but this is not the time for thinking – this is the time for *acting*!'

Nobody's ever talked to me like that before, not even Nan.

I swallow. She keeps her eyes level on me and folds her arms.

'I don't know what he'll be like,' I whisper. 'What if he's like Nan – just a ghost, all thin and disappearing? What if he doesn't know me? What if he hates me?'

'He *doesn't* know you,' she says. 'But I do, and Yanny does. You can do this. Not because of legends, or Lost Princesses. But because you're *you*!'

Her words reach into me, and moments later, nerves

steeled, we rush together towards the palace, ignoring the howl of the shadow creatures around us, and when I strike at the ice that screens the vast front door, it's not that I *think* I can break it with one small fist – or two . . . or even with four, when Zara's join mine – but that I know we *will*. The frozen barrier shatters and crumbles before us, crashing down the steps in a great glacial tide. Sweeping over the icy rubble, I grab the tarnished silver door latch and twist it, desperately muttering the words for the charms that Nan taught me, over and over.

I catch my breath as the door swings open to another wilderness, gleaming ice roping through tarnished silver chandeliers, frozen spider webs clinging to the marble banisters, fine snow carpeting the glass floor.

It used to glow with the amber reflection of candlelight and faelight, and with all the footsteps of all the fae. I lay on it once, to feel the vibrations of all their comings and goings, to feel the bare skin of my arms against its smooth warmth . . .

The memory hits me and slows my footsteps. When I blink it away, the Stag is here, standing before us, his great antlers twisting up and out to fill the vast, bleak hallway. Teacake rushes down the stairs towards us, as the Stag flickers and disappears from view, and the tread of heavy, slow footprints echoes through the palace.

The Shadow King.

'What did your Nan say about breaking the curse?' Zara whispers. 'What do we do now?'

'We were looking for the palace,' I reply. 'And we found it, but there's something . . .' My eyes drift to the stairs that Teacake just came down. 'I think there's something up there.'

'KITTEN!' roars a voice, splitting the air and sending blasts of icy mist through the corridors ahead of us. 'Where have you gone now? I thought you had returned to me!'

We stare at Teacake, who is perched on the marble sphere at the base of the banister. She lifts one front paw and begins to lick it. And I remember. I remember her sitting exactly there, doing exactly this. Only the sun was streaming through the open doors behind me, and my mother was laughing, because she had surprised me so.

'This is Thalia,' she says, lifting me to meet the kitten face to face. 'I found her in the forest, and she followed me home.'

'I thought we said no pets,' rumbles my father, stalking down the steps frowning at the kitten.

'Not a pet,' says my mother, raising her eyes to his. 'Far more than a pet, my dear, which you would know if you'd take the time to look closer. Besides, she chose me. As feline things will. And she will be a perfect playmate for Estelle.'

'Stella?' Zara whispers. 'Shouldn't we stay down here and face him?'

I swallow the lump in my throat. Memories come easy as clouds here, and every time they do, I lose my focus, and forget about Yanny, and what we are doing here. Is that part of the curse? I clear my mind, and something calls to me. The acorn at my throat is warm, and it's pulling me onward.

'Not yet. We need to go up,' I say. 'Teacake, will you distract him down here?'

She blinks, and drops to the floor, venturing down the central corridor.

The steps are slippery blocks of ice, and they seem to go on for miles. We stare up at them, clutching at the bitterly cold banister. I mutter a few words of magic, and as I step forward, the ice melts beneath my feet.

'Step where I've stepped,' I whisper to Zara.

'Magical footsteps!'

'Just . . . melting ice. That's all,' I say. 'Actually, it's making it pretty clear where we've been, isn't it?'

At the top of the steps, we look back to see small footprints leading to where we now stand.

'Let's get rid of them.' I gesture at the staircase, recalling the Latin word for melt. '*Liquescimus!*'

The stairs begin to drip, and the great arches of ice on the chandeliers below us glisten with melting ice. I forge on, Zara by my side, and we tread down the corridor over worn, faded carpet that glitters with frost, and my ears are stretched with listening for him, but there is only silence below.

And then the air is torn by the unmistakeable sound of dawn breaking. I frown.

'It isn't dawn. Is it? We can't have been gone a whole day and night!'

'No, it's not dawn,' Zara says, shifting her feet. 'I need to go, Stella.'

'What?'

'Mrs Mandrake told me it might happen, if things ever went truly badly in Winterspell. I went to see her after I left you yesterday. I still had her number . . . She said Rory would use the horn if she had to – it means there's trouble. You've got this.' She looks at me. 'Really. You have.'

'But shall I come too? What if it's Yanny?'

'What if it is?' she asks. 'You do your bit; I'll do mine. And I promise, Stella, I'll explain later!'

She turns and runs back to the stairs, and I go to shout out after her but a new memory assails me.

'Estelle.' My mother's voice, but pale and worn. Her face, but too thin. Standing by her bed, my hands clutching the cold sheets as someone pulls me away. Screaming. 'My star!' She struggles to sit and uses the last of her fire to drown out my wails. 'Go with your nan. Live your life away from this, and when you are strong and bold, when you are grown, then you will come into your own. Then you will return.' She reaches for the table by the bed, picks up the links of the copper chain and ties it around my neck with a whisper of words that seals it. A single silver acorn hangs at my throat.

I reach for it now, feel the heat of the golden one that has joined it – that hung at her own neck, so long ago – and I force myself onward, down almost familiar corridors, with the sense of her by my side, searching every inch for what I need.

Now I know – there were three acorns. One silver, one gold, and one of rich, dark amber.

The silver light of my cracked fae lantern casts swinging shadows all around me as I start to search in earnest. Every sound echoes. Giant swathes of cobweb drape from every lintel and hang like silent ghosts from the dull pewter chandelier on the landing, and the dust on the floor has been swept to the sides by giant scuffing footsteps.

In the eerie half-light, the palace feels like a cathedral. Every room a vast, echoing chamber with minimal wood furniture and unravelling tapestries on the walls. I work my way back, and the rooms get smaller. In one, there's a row of pitted kettles and old pans hanging from hooks, and a fire pit in the centre with a fat copper pot sitting on a metal rack. Another is heaped with old blankets and cushions, stubs of candles set on the mantelpiece amid old wax spills that drip to the hearth.

I head up again and find threadbare rugs on the cold wood floors, and tatters of curtains hanging at the empty window frames. It's dusty up here, and the air is bitter. Room after room, I catch flashes of the lives that were here before. Rickety old beds, window seats where nobody has sat for years. There's a piano in one room, surrounded by narrow upholstered benches; and in another, a heavy wood dresser. The drawers squeak as I pull them out to reveal neatly folded moth-eaten linen.

'I can't go through *everything*,' I whisper to myself

despairingly, as the next door opens on to yet another room, this one with vast oak wardrobes and a heavily laden bed. I sigh, abandoning the room and trudging to the next.

It's a smaller bedroom that connects to the previous one with a little doorway in the corner. And it's *chaos*. The room, under all the dust and debris, has been torn apart. A chest of drawers lies on its back, its legs broken; its drawers have been ripped out and lie in a pile of wooden shards beside it. A tiny bed has been snapped clean in half, its boards like jagged teeth.

I swing the lantern about me, catching my breath at the destruction it reveals. Something winks in the fireplace. I hold my breath and move towards it, as my vision flickers with what this room might have been like before it was destroyed. The bed beneath the window, heaped with blankets and pillows; the chest of drawers spilling soft clothes. A thick, intricately patterned rug on the floor, and an iron guard up against a gently flickering fire. My mother's voice, and the sound of laughter. My father's broad smile as he reaches down for me, the amber acorn glowing at his neck.

The vision clears as I reach the empty fireplace. Empty, but for a single acorn, almost hidden by a thick pile of ash. I pull it out, and dust drifts through the grate to the floor. A fragment of charred, blackened chain falls from the loop on the top of the acorn to join the ash, and I don't try to rescue it. The acorn is enough. It is the one he wore, of rich dark amber, still warm between my fingers.

I fold it into my palm, and my throat tightens, a sharp cough exploding from my chest. My eyes are burning; my skin stings all over. I bring the amber acorn to the one at my neck, and I feel again that magnetic pull as it merges with them, threading a fine strand of amber through the heart of the silver and gold.

A bolt of something rushes through me, something wrenches and falls apart, and I stumble, catching myself on the wall. Nan's glamour, unspooling as my own power takes over. It's thunder in my veins, but there's no time – there are footsteps on the stairs, heavy as mountains falling, quick as a river, coming towards me . . . The Shadow King himself stalks into the room. There's no time to hide or run – I didn't prepare myself for this. I never even really imagined being in the same room as him. The sheer physical presence of the fae king, so close I could touch him, is a shock that makes the hairs on my arms stand up.

'What do you here?' he asks in a cracking voice. The hair that escapes his hood is long and lank; his beard reaches to his waist in scraggly wisps. He wears threadbare grey robes, drawn in over his thin waist by a knotted leather belt. He comes towards me, and the shadow curls at his side as if trying to get away, but my father fights and wins, and finally. Finally. He is there before me.

Ellos. The Stag. My father.

'Amara?' he whispers, with a dusty, broken voice.

I cannot speak. I just stare at him.

'But no,' he whispers, as if to himself, one claw-like hand on the door, pulling himself upright. 'No, I watched her die. And the sickness was tight in my belly, and I could not be sure . . . I thought I had imagined my mother there. She took . . . something. I forget. What did she take? What are you?'

'She took me,' I say, and I weld my voice with steel so that it does not shake. 'She took me away from the Plaga – and your shadows. And we tried to come back to you, but you had locked yourself up here . . .' I gesture around us, while ice drips, and the sun's pale wintry rays begin to filter through windows. 'And you had cursed the whole place, sent your shadows so far and wide, given them so much power, there was no way through.'

'My daughter.' He nods absently, his eyes still turned inward. 'I remember we had a daughter. I did not know where she had gone, whether she survived the sickness at all. I sent out my stag to find her, but they said she had gone with her mother.'

'Who said?'

'The . . . the shadows . . .'

'And you listened? You listened to your own shadows? Your own fears?'

He blinks, and it is as though he hasn't blinked for a thousand years. For a million lifetimes. Brown eyes, crinkled at the corners, desperately confused. He takes a step forward; I take one back. The acorn gleams at my neck, and he sees it.

'Estelle? You do look like Amara. Except for the horns. Those are mine.' He reaches thin, brittle fingers up to touch the horns, half hidden in the thatch of his brown-grey hair, and I do the same.

I gasp. . . Horns. Smooth as new conkers, spiralling like shells.

I have *horns*.

'What do you want from me?' the Shadow King asks,

furrowing his brow. 'Why are you here? Why do you interrupt my silence? My peace?'

My stomach twists. I cannot work out whether he is still confused or just angry that I'm here. Has he really searched for me, or does he think I died with my mother? Does he think I'm just a dream?

'I . . . want you to stop the shadows,' I manage finally.

'I cannot stop them!'

'You made them! So make them go away!'

'I . . . I made them?'

'And they are destroying Winterspell. Killing trees. Killing fae.'

'But no. They do not . . . They are not for the forest! I thought they were mine alone. They were my punishment, for I let my lady die, and I lost our child. I have been haunted by them. First the Stag – I could not control him, once he had grown strong in my sorrow. And from him, so many others came. I could not see past them. Could not leave this place!'

'It wasn't just you they affected – it was the whole of Winterspell! You didn't see how they struggled? How they fought?'

'Fae always fight.' He shrugs. 'That is what they are. It is what they live for.'

'Not for fighting with shadows,' I say.

'I did not see that. I have been locked in this palace, lost in the shadows. But who are you to say such things?' he demands, and his eyes, when I find the courage to look into them again, barely see me at all. They are dull once more, as if they see nothing. Nothing but the shadows of his despair, of his own personal agony.

That which has caused the misery of so many.

One person's fear. One person's misery.

A whole world near-destroyed.

'Who are *you* to come into *my* palace?'

The shadows swing, and another pane of the glass in my lantern cracks. The light gutters and snuffs out. We are plunged into darkness.

'Well, child?' whispers the Shadow King, leaning in, so close I can see his long grey teeth and smell his rotten breath. 'Brave, or stupid? What do you think?'

'Neither,' I snap.

He draws closer still, and the acorn at my throat begins to burn.

'Get away from me!'

He laughs, a horrible creaking, gasping sound, and rocks back on his heels, thrusting out a bony arm to gesture around the room. My eyes adjust to the gloom. In the corners, and crawling up the old glass window, are his infernal shadows. They twist through the doorway, hang from the picture rails, and their forms are not solid. In here, they are not animals or men, but things that undulate and morph, that speak in slithery, slippery tones of fear and malice.

'Get away?' snarls the Shadow King. 'You are in *my* domain! You have entered this place of your own free will – for what? For battle?' He grins. 'You will not win, small thing. You *cannot* win, here, for my will is greater than yours, and I have nothing to lose. There is nothing you can do to me, nothing you can offer me. This palace is mine, and if Winterspell is lost, there is nothing I can do about it. Nature will take its course.'

'Nature?' I breathe through the creep, swallowing all my fear. 'You cannot talk of nature when all you've done is destroy it. Winterspell is not yours – can't you feel that? Can't you sense the trees themselves are against you? The fae, who hide from you? What are you ruling, apart from your own shadows?'

He roars, and I thrust out my hands as if I can push him back. The acorn bursts with a golden light as the thundering feeling of magic explodes in my chest, and it becomes a tiny beacon that spears through the shadows and sends them reeling.

The Shadow King stumbles back.

'Estelle,' he whispers, raising one hand to shield his eyes.

'Stop them!' I shout.

'I don't know how.'

I stare at him with hollow, dry eyes, and something deep inside me breaks. The part of me that carried just a little hope for all these years; that I would find him, and that he would welcome me.

That I would have a father.

My body is trembling – with rage or fear, I cannot tell.

'Fine. Then I'll do it myself.'

I stalk past him, down the stairs and out of the melting palace. The shadows pursue me as I go; surrounding me, looming dark over my head. But they cannot stop me now.

They cannot get close enough to try.

28

The clearing where I left Yanny alone is a now a calamitous battle scene. Rory is there, sending arrows of pure light into the shadows that smother the trees, and a dozen more centaurs cluster around her, doing the same. The shadows have completely surrounded the clearing.

I venture closer, looking for Yanny and Zara, but there's too much going on. Sprites up in the trees, battling with spells and flashing eyes; fairies on light feet, fighting great shadow monsters with enchanted swords and knives; Mr Flint is standing close by a group of young fae, roaring as he flourishes a long, grey staff, crashing into a pack of shadow wolves, which snap at their heels. As I watch, one of the creatures gathers itself and launches at him; he parries with a swish of his staff, and the wolf is torn into ragged patches of shadow that drift upward to rejoin the dark mass gathered over the trees.

It's impossible, I realize. All they're doing is driving the shadows back into the woods, where they'll infect the trees. And I told my father I would stop them, but I still haven't worked that bit out. I wanted to reach him. I wanted him to see me and be fixed.

'Stupid,' I mutter to myself, treading out into the clearing, catching sight of Peg in the distance, clinging to a tree and sending bolts of fire down through the dark clouds of shadow. It's dusk already, somehow a whole winter's day has passed, and the dangers of night can't be far off. 'Stupid. Just made it worse. Now what, oh Lost Prince?'

'*Lost Prince?*' says a small voice, deep inside my head. '*Is that what you'll call yourself, even now that you are found?*'

I look around. Nobody has noticed me yet, this whole part of the clearing is completely empty, apart from the shadows that crouch just outside of my reach. Something furry lands on my shoulder, making me jump.

'Teacake?' I twist my head.

I found you, she purrs.

She speaks. She speaks, and I understand her. My jaw slackens as I gaze into her bright green eyes.

And you found your father. Teacake rubs against my

276

cheek. *So you are not lost. Your body knows it before your mind does.*

She whisks at me with her tail, and I'm reminded of my new horns. My hair, I notice, is also different. I pull a strand outward to inspect it. It curls, flecked with streaks of copper.

The question is . . . Teacake purrs. *What will you do now that you are found?*

I stare at her for a long moment, and then I remember the voice I heard the first time I fought the shadow, in the garden. Was it hers?

'I wanted to get rid of the shadows,' I say, still marvelling at her.

That is a good idea, she continues. *I am tired of them. So is your father – though he doesn't know it yet.*

'He didn't know me.'

He has been a long time in shadows.

'He made the shadows!'

Do you think he made them of his own volition? Did he choose this life? No. It came upon him, and he was lost. It happens. What you will do with your life, Stella. That is the interesting bit.

'Is it?'

Somewhat – she licks a paw – *I cannot quite read it.*

Some things are not clear until they are upon us. Ooh! A lovely little mouse, hiding in the snow . . .

She bounds off into the trees, and I watch her go before turning back to the clearing, where fae face shadows. Neither side appears to be winning. Now I understand those flashes of light and colour that I used to see from our house. Now I am close to the roars, and the screams of the centaurs as they charge, and the sparks that fly off their weapons, bursting into the air as the fairies use their magic.

There are goblins fighting tooth and nail with spiny shadow creatures, and sprites who lean out from every tree, using their magic and their swords to fend off the shadow birds, which try to land on the outstretched frost-glinting branches. And there is Yanny, back to back with Zara, fighting a group of shadow foxes. Yanny is quick with his fire whip, it sparks as it snaps the ground, and Zara is wielding what looks like a long glass rod, glowing blue from within.

Is that what she went to see Mrs Mandrake about? To get herself a weapon? While I've been faffing about, she's already begun the fight. There is no time to lose; I have wasted enough already. I run over to them.

'Stella!' Zara grins. 'Are you ready?' Her breath is short. 'You look . . . ready.'

Her gaze settles on my newly revealed horns, and then travels down over my bright hair.

'And you've brought company,' says Yanny, with a flourish of his whip that parts the shadows at my back. 'I'm not sure we needed more of them!'

'He wouldn't send them away,' I say. 'So I told him I'd do it instead.'

'Best get started then,' he grunts, as one of the foxes gets too close and rakes its claws at his shoulder.

I clatter at it with Nan's old lantern, and the fox fragments into a dozen pieces, which begin to crawl and slither as soon as they hit the ground.

'OK?' I manage, as the next thing is upon us.

Yanny winces. 'I'll be fine . . . I'm not sure about *your* fighting methods though.' He watches as I swing the lantern again, this time into a swooping shadow owl.

'I didn't bring any other weapons!'

'Some Lost Prince you are.'

'Not a Lost Prince!' I huff, swirling the lantern through the shadow snakes that now gather by our ankles. 'Just me. Stella Brigg.'

I flail and batter with my lantern, aware of its

absurdity. It does seem to be working, though. The air around us starts to clear, and the shadows that get hit by the lantern are slow to re-form; some of them disappear entirely.

'You're pretty handy with that!' yells Zara, swiping up with her spear to catch a small spine-covered shadow that has launched itself from the nearest tree.

I grin. 'Could say the same for you!'

'Mrs Mandrake gave it to me,' she says, wielding the spear with a flourish and accidentally catching a shadow bat that was coming close in behind her. 'She said if I heard the horn, it would be time. I don't think she thought it would happen so soon . . .'

Her voice drifts off, and she looks with horror over my shoulder into the distance.

I turn slowly, and my stomach fills with icy dread.

He is here, approaching slowly through the frigid reaches of the forest where the palace hides. The Stag. And behind him, a horde of terrible shadows I've not seen before, all of them gruesome monsters nearly ten feet tall.

'You must've made him angry,' Yanny says. His whip is smouldering, his eyes no longer ablaze.

I gasp. 'It wasn't just a scratch!' I pull him away from

the shadows to take a closer look at his shoulder. The cloth of his shirt is torn, and beneath is what looks like an ugly burn. 'Yanny, you need to get this seen to!'

'Get your father seen to first!'

'This is more important right now, Yanny! Where are your parents? Who's the healer around here? Quickly!'

'Hang on!' says Zara, dipping into the pocket of her yellow mac. Camouflaged, she is not. 'Don't panic, Mrs Mandrake gave me this . . .'

She brings out a small glass jar, the label of which reads *Mrs M's Best Blackcurrant Jam*.

'What *is* that?' Yanny scowls, wrinkling his nose as she unscrews the lid. 'I don't think this is the time for Mrs M's Best Blackcurrant Jam!'

'It's not jam.' Zara rolls her eyes. 'It's mer-fae nest, mixed with some other bits and bobs. Have you ever seen Mrs Mandrake's house? It's amazing – shelf after shelf of jars and rocks and potions. This is a new thing – she made it up after she fixed you that day . . . Anyway, she said it might help if anyone was injured.' Zara dips a finger into the jar, and leans over Yanny, smearing it on his shoulder before he has a chance to move away.

'There,' she says.

'It stings!'

'Good medicine always stings,' she says, tucking the jar back into her pocket. 'Or tastes vile. At least I didn't make you eat it!'

I turn back to the Stag, who is coming over the icy ground, taking his majestic time as the shadows grow longer with nightfall. 'Is it helping, Yanny?' I ask urgently.

'Probably,' he says, shifting his shoulder.

'You can thank me later,' Zara says. 'Once we've sorted this guy out.'

She bares her teeth in a growl, standing up and glaring at the Stag.

'Zara!'

'He's making me cross,' she says. 'Look at him, prancing along as if he owns the place, after everything he's done.' She turns to me. 'Aren't you angry, Stella?'

'Sad.'

'Be sad later,' she says. 'Angry now.'

Yanny and I stare at her, but all she does is shrug.

'Isn't it time?' she says.

'I'd say so,' says Yanny, looking over at the place where his parents stand shoulder to shoulder, battling shadow men with bolts and chains of fire.

Rory turns from the melee and sees us. She charges

over, the shadows thick in her wake. They cling tight to her night-dark flanks, and they spool from her hooves as she thunders towards us. And then Peg is here, rushing up to my shoulder, a tiny glowing lizard.

'Oh, Peg,' I whisper, as Rory halts, sending up a flurry of ice crystals.

'You know how to do it! We practised in the garden,' Peg says. 'Don't you remember?'

'That was practice? I thought it was an emergency!'

'It was both,' he says, somehow managing to sound smug even in the midst of all this chaos. 'And now that you are come into your power, you will be magnificent!'

'She is a child, foolish imp,' snaps Rory, leaning towards us. 'What do you propose she do? I never bought into that ridiculous legend – it means nothing on the battlefield. She is a child, barely versed in our world.'

'I have been to the palace,' I say. 'I fought through the shadows and the deepest part of the forest, and I faced my father, and he didn't know me, or if he did, it was only for a moment. He is lost, but I am not.' I remember Teacake's words and let them ring true. 'I'm right here. And I want to help.'

'She can do it,' says Yanny, and his voice sends a rush of hope through me as he stands by my side.

And then Zara is here too. And if Yanny is tired and fading, then she has only just begun. Her eyes spark; she looks ready to take on the whole of Winterspell by herself.

Rory snorts. 'Go on, then. Show me what magic you have.'

'I don't think this lantern is going to do much against him,' I whisper to Yanny, as the Stag raises his head and bellows through the clearing.

'It's not the flipping lantern,' he says, shaking his head. 'It's never the *stuff* that matters, Stella. It's what you put into it! The lantern is just an extension of your hand – of your power. The lantern isn't sending shadows away – you are! Just . . . do it bigger!'

'Send him away, Stella,' Zara says, tucking her arm through mine.

Yanny links my arm on the other side, a look of determination on his face. And something clicks, deep inside me. Something that was so lonely, and even today, standing before my father, felt so out of place.

I'm not out of place.

I'm not alone.

I am fae. I am all that he is, and more, because I have

friends, and he stands alone in a flurry of nothing but his own fear.

I breathe long and slow, and let it gather, noticing that the clearing has become still. Every fae creature is staring from me to the Stag. Fierce Elowen is shouting something, but I cannot hear the words through the snarling chaos. The Stag stands before me, his breath steaming, antlers held high, and he roars, and I take a step towards him, and my bare feet don't make a sound on the ground, and I clench my fists, and I roar right back at him, and it reverberates, a boom of sound that never came from a human mouth. I pour all of my hurt in there, and all of my fear, until my chest burns, until my back aches. The acorn at my neck flashes hot, and then there is a sharp twist of pain, and a lift beneath my ribs. My heart is thudding like a thunderstorm. I look at the shadow of my father, who does not acknowledge me, even now.

'Get *away* from here,' I say in a small voice that somehow rings through the clearing, as the moon comes into view, crescent-thin and dazzling bright.

He lowers his head as if preparing to charge, and I step towards him again, and I start to run, but the ground falls away beneath my feet as wings – *my* wings, that Nan's glamour hid for all these years – spread and catch the air, and Winterspell lights up around me.

Every tree and leaf, every bright face and every single fae form is caught in a silver burst of light, until the clearing is a dazzle of outstretched, beating wings. They sweep out from the backs of all the cursed young fairies and sprites in a rainbow torch of magic, and the shadows cannot stand beneath such light. They don't just rush to shelter. They don't yammer or growl or fight. They simply stretch to tatters and disappear.

The willow trees lower their heads, the rowan spread their limbs, the fae stamp their feet, and the shadow of the Stag is massive. He is all of them in one place, just one creature with no more or less power than any other.

'Go back to him!' I shout.

The clearing rings with it, and my heart thunders as I stare at him. He looks at me then, right in the eye, and finally he nods. He turns, making his way back to the palace that is no longer hidden.

'You did it!' crows Yanny.

'My,' whispers Rory. 'Look at that.'

Zara slips her hand into mine. 'You cleared the shadows.'

'I sent the Stag away. I sent him,' I shiver, the cold

finding its way to my bones. The air is crisp, everything more stark than it was a moment ago, before the shadows fled. 'Will it kill him, Zara?'

'No,' says Peg, the familiar curve of his bird claws digging into my shoulder. 'You used the power of your family, and your own, more importantly, and you sent his shadow back to him.' His face looms before mine, his amber eyes glowing, a massive grin on his imp face. 'You sent the shadows away – you broke the curse, Stella!'

'What?'

I look up. Rory and her centaurs are staring at me, the fairies and the sprites too.

'The Stag was the source of it all, and you sent it back to where it belonged,' Rory says. 'To your father.'

'And you have wings!' Yanny rushes at me, and he isn't tired any more – he is flying, his own wings no longer tattered shadows but huge great sweeps of fire at his back. He curls up into the air, and then he swoops back down and flings me up with him, and I'm tumbling, diving, catching myself at the last minute, soaring in a flurry of fae wings, so many of them all whooping and hollering beneath the moon.

They are so sure of it. So full of joy. I twist and dive with them, and it should feel like a dream. Like magic.

But I cannot see my own wings, and I don't trust them fully. I don't know what I've done. I don't know who I am, and there's a weight in my throat that doesn't shift, no matter how their joy rings. I stumble to the ground, where Zara is grinning, leaning against her staff.

'Look at you,' I say, climbing to my feet. 'All fae and magical.'

'Says she with the wings.' She grins.

'He didn't want me there, Zara,' I say, watching the fairies and the sprites flit through the night sky.

It's clear now. No clouds, no shadows.

She huffs. 'Well, more fool him.'

I snort back a weird laughing crying cough.

'Really though,' she says. 'This is your life. You're living it the best you can.' She shrugs. 'Your best is pretty spectacular. But even if it wasn't, it would be fine, Stella. It'd be good enough for us. Even if it isn't for him.'

We link arms and look up together as Yanny curls through the air. He hollers, waving down at us, and does a pirouette in the air, falling and landing clumsily. Elowen darts forward and takes his face in her hands, and she is laughing, her wings unfolding as he pulls her off her feet and back up into the sky with him.

29

'I think,' Rory says, 'that it's time for us to go and see your grandmother.'

I nod, with a sidelong look at Zara, and then we make our way through Winterspell, Peg on my shoulder.

The stars are clear now, sparkling brightly between the branches, and as we go, I can hear the trees whispering. I trail my fingers along their trunks, and they speak to me of long summer days to come, and bright, moonlit nights, and the play of fae children in their arms. The air is singing with it, and even Rory seems somewhat mollified by the time we come out the other side with Zara and Mrs Mandrake.

'We'll let you chat to your nan,' Mrs Mandrake says as we near the house. 'I'll see Zara home.'

'Is that OK?' I ask Zara, as Mrs Mandrake skirts the house to her truck. 'You can come in . . .'

'I think I'll leave that pleasure to you,' she says,

her eyes sparkling. 'I want to talk to Mrs Mandrake anyway.'

'I'm so glad you were there,' I say, drawing her in for a hug.

Zara smiles. 'We did a pretty good job in there, didn't we? And Mrs Mandrake says that now I've seen so much, I'll have to sign the secret contract thing and have lessons with you upstairs!'

I grin back, revelling at the prospect – but the elation is short-lived.

'When you've finished congratulating yourselves, girls,' says Rory, shifting her hooves. 'Perhaps we could proceed?'

Zara shoots me a look of sympathy and darts around the house to the waiting truck . . . It's very tempting to go with her.

'Come, Stella,' says Rory. 'Undo these cursed charms – they're hurting my eyes.'

I turn to the charms along the silver wire and run my fingers along them, whispering the words of undoing. Wondering if we'll need them again. Then Nan is at the door, and Rory is lowering her head to get through.

'Perhaps I should go back into Winterspell,' says Peg. 'Just to check things are still OK . . .'

'Ha, no!' I say. 'If I've got to go in the house, so have you. Besides, Nan will have been worrying.'

We head in, Teacake dashing in before us and making for the hearth.

'Well, what a fine nest you made for yourself,' says Rory to Nan as she ushers us in.

Having a centauride in your kitchen is no laughing matter. But after a frosty start, she and Nan start to talk in earnest, and the tension slowly ebbs away. They speak of the palace, now clear for all to see, and the thaw of my father's winter. There is talk of him facing trial, of banishment. I sit with Peg and Teacake, trying not to think too hard about any of it. My head is thrumming with everything that's happened, and my wings shift restlessly at my back. They feel weird.

I stand to look in the mirror over the fireplace.

My father's copper-flashing strands of hair are woven through the brown, now. My mother's silver, mirror eyes. The horns, that do look a little like spiralling conkers, set high on my brow. And the wings. I turn to study them. They gleam with bright curling lines of silver and copper.

I am fae. Truly fae: half moon sprite and half wood sprite.

'Do you like the look of yourself?' says Rory, her eyes laughing.

'I think I do,' I say.

Nan nods. 'As you should. I'd forgotten how lovely your wings are. Rather unusual to have such elements combined.'

'She's rather unusual all round, I should say,' says Rory. 'I may have underestimated her. She broke her father's curse, legend or no legend.'

It's late, and my eyes are scratchy with tiredness, but I can't make myself move. Rory said her goodbyes hours ago, and so it's just me and Nan, and Peg and Teacake. Home. Safe. Everything the same, and yet . . . everything different.

'I thought he would help, Nan,' I say, looking into the fire.

'I know you did.' She sighs. 'Of course you did.'

'You warned me he wouldn't. You said he was lost, but I thought . . . I thought that if he just *saw* me, he would find himself. But he didn't even really *see* me. He just stood there . . . and I had to go and do it myself.'

'But Stella – you *did* do it.' She wedges herself next to me on the bench and puts her hand over mine. 'You went in there, and you came back out again, and you fought. And you won.'

'It doesn't *feel* like we won,' I say.

'Give it time,' she says. 'This is just the start, Stella.'

'What will happen to him? And the palace – will we go back there, Nan?'

'If we want to, in time,' she says. And then she sneezes.

'Nan!'

'Bother that cat.' She frowns, glaring at Teacake, who rolls over to show us her pale belly.

'She was in the palace, Nan,' I say, reaching out to tickle Teacake. 'My mother brought her home for me, before she died.'

'I knew there was something about her,' Nan says, staring more closely. 'Rory has a theory about her too.'

'What's that?'

'She thinks she may be a sphynx. Future-seeing, wise, you know. A creature of legend.'

Peg cackles from the mantelpiece.

'A creature of legend.' I smile. 'That sounds about right. She spoke to me in Winterspell – and I understood.'

'She's been speaking to you for longer than that,' says Peg, propping himself up on one arm. 'Going on all the time – only you couldn't hear it through that glamour of Nan's. She's still just a silly kitten though.'

'From tiny acorns . . .' teases Nan with a smile. 'They aren't born old and wise, after all. Nothing is.' She puts an arm around me. Her cardigan is worn and thin, her white hair tickles my nose.

'Nan! I can feel you!' I say. 'You're all solid!'

Peg grins. 'It's taken you long enough to figure that out!'

'Oh!' Nan says, holding out her hands and examining them. 'Well so I am!'

'How did that happen?'

'I don't rightly know,' she says, her eyes gleaming in the firelight.

'It's because Stella broke the spell,' Peg says, speaking very slowly as if we're very stupid. 'All those years glamouring the house – and you, Stella – the energy had to come from somewhere. It came from you. And now it's back!'

'That . . . would make sense,' says Nan, stretching out her feet to admire them.

'Are you still a ghost?' I ask.

'Oh yes,' she says. 'Only now, I'm a little more substantial. And I,' she says grandly, sweeping up and over to the kitchen, 'am going to make us all a lovely healthy dinner. And then I'll feed the chickens, and then . . . I'm going to read a book.'

Peg grimaces as Nan reaches for the dusty jar of lentils at the back of the worktop, whistling under her breath. I grin at him. I'd eat lentils every day for the rest of my life if I could hear her whistling while she does it.

Well.

Nearly every day.

Acknowledgments

I wrote *Shadows of Winterspell* at a time of great change and loss for our family, and there were times I felt as alone and as roarish as the stag himself. But. I wasn't.

I'm very grateful for all of the people who have shown such kindness over this last year, and over the last four books, and always.

Firstly I'm thankful to my agent, Amber Caraveo, who takes such dreadful synopses and pushes them until they're actually a fully formed story, and for so much more besides. I'm thankful to my editor Lucy, for all her faith and wise, gently steering words. I'm thankful to my publicist Jo Hardacre, for getting me out and about, and to all three of them, and everybody else at Macmillan Children's, to Sabina, Cate, Amber, Jess, Kat, Alyx et al., for kindness, and for general heroism, and flowers, and proofs. And cake.

I'm thankful to all of the librarians, teachers and booksellers who work so tirelessly and with such passion at such trying times, and I'm thankful to all of my fellow authors, for reading and shouting and for being such wonderful, passionate inspirations. I know I'd not be where I am without you.

Special thanks to Caroline, Aviva, and Lu, I am honoured to call you friends, thanks to Judith, and Charles, and thanks without bounds to my husband Lee, and to our children Theia, Aubrey, and Sasha, and to Rocky too, for laughter and silliness and hugs and stories and love. So much love.

Here is love, now, to my childhood family. To my father Harry Berry - how we have missed you. To my brother Matt, who we lost too soon. We play your piano, and treasure your hat, though it's too small for my head. To my mother, Helen, whose love is fierce and strong and constant as she has been. You will always be an inspiration, to all of us. To my sister Hannah, who is precious and brave and who has been through so much with me, and to Mike, whose own love has been such a gift.

And here is love to you, dear reader - without you, my words would be pickling around in a tortured word document, or worse, in my head! I'm grateful for every book you buy, borrow, lend, review, or mention in passing. I hope you will always find the adventure you need, just when you need it.

Turn the page for an extract of
Amy Wilson's exciting novel,
Snowglobe

'Literally spellbinding' Piers Torday

Prologue

There were three sisters, named for Jupiter's moons: Ganymede, Callisto and Io. As they had blood in their veins, so they had magic, fine and strong as a spider's web. They lived in a house of white marble, and the tower stretched to the sky and speared the clouds, searching, they said, for the moon. They filled it with miniature worlds, set whole galaxies spinning, caught within glass spheres. And then they hid in their house while the world changed.

That was their lot.

But lots can change, and change can be chaos.

Callisto was the first to go: she left for love and the laughter of a boy with hair as red as fire.

Io was next: she left for solitude, and found her home in a place none could ever change.

Ganymede was left alone in the house of infinity. She stalked the marble corridors, ruling over everything they had created with a hard eye.

The world never knew of these sisters. Their house went unseen, their stories unheard.

And then came chaos.

1

It's not like it's hurting. Not much. And the lesson is only ten minutes longer – I've been watching the clock – so he'll have to stop soon anyway. I try to ignore it, but it's *prod, prod*, at the base of my spine. *Prod, prod*, like a heartbeat, only not so regular.

It's science, and we're sitting on stools, so it doesn't take much for him to reach back from the bench behind and do it. One, two, *prod, prod*. I find myself counting the seconds between them. Ten, eleven, perhaps he's forgotten – *prod, prod*. Thirteen, fourteen, fifteen, *prod*.

I don't know why he took such a dislike to me. It was pretty instant, I remember, on the first day of school. He looked at me; I looked back at him. I tried a smile, but he turned and said something to his friend, and they both began to laugh. It took me a few seconds to realize the laughter was unkind, and the smile froze on my face, heat rushed to my cheeks and they laughed harder. They laughed at everything then. My clothes, my bag, my hair. He said my eyes were weird; that all of me was weird. I went in every morning trying not to be, hoping it'd be different. New bag, bright smile, same eyes – no difference. What was worse, he turned the laughter on to anyone who sat by me. Nobody sits by me now, except those who are made to in lessons.

It's OK. I read my books, smile at the new kids, hope, hope, it'll change.

It hasn't, so far. Doesn't matter how bright I make my smile; the weirdness shines brighter, I guess.

Mrs Elliott is talking about the homework, and I'm behind already, so I should focus. I try to listen, but *prod, prod* – it's all I can hear now, all I even am. It is *my* heartbeat, *prod, prod*, faltering and mean, *prod*. She's saying something about force, *prod*. And then there's a whisper, and a breath of laughter, and something breaks deep inside me, like a wishbone that's been pulled too tight and shattered into pieces.

'*STOP!*' I howl, whirling from my stool to face him just as he reaches out his arm again. I push it away and something flashes, bright as lightning. His stool ricochets across the science lab, and he flies with it.

There's a terrible crashing racket as he and the stool land up at the far wall, and then a deafening silence. My ears are ringing; my head feels like it's been pressed in a vice.

'*Clementine Gravett!*' shouts Mrs Elliott. 'Mrs Duke's office, immediately!'

She charges over to Jago, who is in a little heap beside the now-broken stool. He stares at me, like he knows something. Like he's got something on me now. Like he knew all along I was a freak, and here's the evidence: he knows that wasn't ordinary; it wasn't just strength. The whole class is silent, and they watch without a word as I pick up my bag and head out of the room.

It was magic.

My mother's magic.

I've been pretending ever since my first day at secondary, ever since Jago first saw the weird in me, that it isn't real. The roar of my blood, the flashes of static – all just the fantasies of a daydreamer. When I was smaller, that was all it was. But ever since my eleventh birthday, it's been getting stronger, less dream-like.

And the last two minutes have changed everything.

*

'Tell me what happened.'

I can see from Mrs Duke's face that she really wants to know. I'm a quiet girl. I don't hit, or shout, or storm out of classrooms. I don't make a fuss. Sometimes my work is scruffy, sometimes my homework is late, and I don't have the best grades, but I'm not a troublemaker.

'I don't know.'

'Clementine, I can't help you if I don't know what's going on. This seems out of character . . .' She leans forward at the waist, looking at me intently. Her expression is so kind. I've never seen her like this before. Her office is pale with winter sun, and dust motes float around us. I hope I'm not swallowing them; I try to breathe through my nose.

'Clementine?'

I can't look her in the eye. I concentrate on the biscuit-coloured carpet and my black boots. They're scuffed, and the yellow laces are unravelling.

'Mrs Elliott was quite shocked,' she continues, resting back into the comfy chair again. We're in the informal bit of the office, away from her desk. The chairs are navy blue and scratchy. Her short silver hair shines in the sunlight coming through the window. 'She says you

306

pushed him clear across the classroom. We were lucky he wasn't injured. *You* were lucky, Clementine.'

'I didn't mean to,' I say.

She sighs. 'But you did. And there are consequences.' She looks up at the clock. 'Your father is on his way. Perhaps we'd better not continue until he arrives.'

'He's coming?'

'We called him.' She nods, watching me closely. 'Is that OK?'

'Yes.'

I don't tell her I'm surprised he's coming; it might not sound right. I love my pa, but he's very absent-minded, and he tends not to do things other parents would do. Like come to school. He hasn't been here in so long I wonder if he'll find it. I wonder what he'll say.

'Mr Gravett, the stool *broke*,' she says some time later, her voice close to despair. 'Clementine is a good student,' her eyes flick over me again, as if to reassure herself that I really am. 'But we can't tolerate violence of any kind, and she has made no explanation.'

'Clem?'

His eyes are sorrowful as ever, his unbrushed hair standing up on end, like a burning match. He doesn't look like he belongs here. I guess neither do I. Maybe that's what Jago saw that first day, a year ago.

'I didn't mean to,' I say.

Mrs Duke sighs, tapping her fingers on the folder she has on her lap.

'I just wanted to stop him.'

'From doing what?'

They both lean in to me. And my mouth dries up. What am I going to say, he poked me in the back? It sounds ridiculous, like I'm five. I suppose I could talk about all the other things that have happened over the last year, but they're all so small, so silly.

He says I'm a freak.

He says it might be catching.

He shoves his chair out and tries to trip me, just as I'm passing with my lunch tray.

No.

I don't know how to explain it. I was different from the start, and it's lonely, even in the moments he's not there to taunt me. Surrounded by hundreds of people every day, and alone all the same. I overhear conversations, and in my head I join in sometimes, smile at a funny bit, and then I realize I'm just staring at people, smiling to myself. Or I have thoughts that want to be out there, and they just wedge in my head because there's nobody to tell them to. Maybe I whisper to myself when I walk along the bustling corridors. Maybe I stare too much at other people. Maybe I drop books, miss balls, stumble on steps, maybe I just don't quite fit. Maybe that's why I bother him so much.

But I don't say any of that.

I don't say anything at all.

Mrs Duke raises her hands at my silence. 'I have no choice, Mr Gravett,' she says. 'Even if Clementine *had* some sort of justification, it wouldn't be enough. We have a zero-tolerance policy, and there is no question that she pushed Jago, hard enough to break his stool and throw him to the floor. She will have to be suspended.'

'Suspended?' Pa asks.

I blush. He probably doesn't even know what that means. He probably thinks they're going to hang me upside down on the nearest tree.

'She is not allowed on to the grounds of this school for two days,' she says, her voice crisp with frustration. 'We will expect her back next Wednesday, and not before. She may access the online portal to get her homework and any study notes.'

Pa blinks, and stares at her.

'I fail to see how that is going to resolve the issue between them.'

'We will have to pick that up on Clementine's return,' she says smoothly. 'I hope that over the intervening period, Clementine will have a chance to work out what *did* happen here today, and be able to articulate it so that we can work with her on a solution.'

Pa mutters something under his breath before springing to his feet. Mrs Duke flinches back into the chair – he doesn't look like he'd be so nimble.

'Come on, Clem,' he says. 'Let's go.'

He doesn't exactly smile at me, but there's a twinkle in his eye as he picks up my bag and swings it over his shoulder.

Mrs Duke stands and follows us out, frowning from the door as we leave – two little matches against a grey sky. We don't look like we fit because, sometimes, we don't. Pa may not have it in his blood, but he's known about magic for longer than I've been alive. And me?

I guess there's not much use in denying it now.

About the Author

Amy Wilson has a background in journalism and lives in Bristol with her family. She is a graduate of the Bath Spa MA in Creative Writing and is the author of the critically acclaimed novels *A Girl Called Owl* – nominated for the CILIP Carnegie medal and longlisted for the Branford Boase Award – *A Far Away Magic* and *Snowglobe*, a W H Smith Travel Book of the Month selection. She also contributed to the *Return to Wonderland* collection of *Alice*-inspired short stories published by Macmillan.